Praise for Dancing Dogs

"Jon Katz's first story collection is sure to win dog-lovers' hearts with its warm, insightful glimpses of life at both ends of the leash." —Shelf Awareness

"The touching stories included in *Dancing Dogs* are sure to stir your emotions. Whether they're lying down or getting into mischief, their love and loyalty is undeniable."

—*Jewish Journal*

Praise for Jon Katz

"With wisdom and grace, Katz unlocks the canine soul and the complicated wonders that lie within and offers powerful insights to anyone who has ever struggled with, and loved, a troubled animal." —John Grogan, author of *Marley & Me*

"Katz's world—of animals and humans and their combined generosity of spirit—is a place you're glad you've been."

—*The Boston Globe*

"From Toto to Marley, our canine friends are a sure bet in the literary biz. But no one seems to speak their language like Jon Katz." —*San Antonio Express-News*

"Katz proves himself a Thoreau for modern times as he ponders the relationships between man and animals, humanity and nature." —Fort Worth *Star-Telegram*

"I toss a lifetime award of three liver snaps to Jon Katz." —MAUREEN CORRIGAN, National Public Radio's *Fresh Air*

"It's always a comfort to read a Jon Katz book." —Minneapolis *Star Tribune*

"Anyone who loves animals or country life, but maybe can't have a pet or actually live in the country, will find Katz a perfect armchair companion." —*Publishers Weekly*

By Jon Katz

The Second-Chance Dog
The Story of Rose (eBook)
Dancing Dogs
Going Home
Rose in a Storm
Soul of a Dog
Izzy & Lenore
Dog Days
A Good Dog
Katz on Dogs
The Dogs of Bedlam Farm
The New Work of Dogs
A Dog Year
Geeks
Running to the Mountain
Virtuous Reality
Media Rants
Sign Off
Death by Station Wagon
The Family Stalker
The Last Housewife
The Fathers' Club
Death Row

Books for Children

Meet the Dogs of Bedlam Farm
Lenore Finds a Friend

Dancing Dogs

Dancing Dogs

| Stories |

JON KATZ

RANDOM HOUSE TRADE PAPERBACKS • NEW YORK

Dancing Dogs is a work of fiction. Names, characters, places, and incidents are the products of the author's imagination or are used fictitiously. Any resemblane to actual events, locales, or persons, living or dead, is entirely coincidental.

2013 Random House Trade Paperback Edition

Published in the United States by Random House Trade Paperbacks, an imprint of The Random House Publishing Group, a division of Random House, Inc., New York.

RANDOM HOUSE TRADE PAPERBACKS and the HOUSE colophon are trademarks of Random House, Inc.

Originally published in hardcover in the United States by Ballantine Books, an imprint of The Random House Publishing Group, a division of Random House, Inc., in 2012.

LIBRARY OF CONGRESS CATALOGING-IN-PUBLICATION DATA

Katz, Jon.
Dancing dogs: stories/ Jon Katz
p. cm.
ISBN 978-0-345-50267-4
eISBN 978-0-345-53616-7
1. Dogs—Fiction. 2. Human–animal relationships—Fiction.
3. Short stories, American. I. Title.
PS3561.A7558D36 2011 813'.54—DC23 2012021478

Printed in the United States of America on acid-free paper

www.atrandom.com

2 4 6 8 9 7 5 3 1

Book design by Susan Turner

For Minnie Cohen

Contents

Dancing Dogs

Gracie's Last Walk

CAROLYN PULLED THE BATTERED OLD BLACK SAMSONITE SUITCASE her father had given her down the stairs at the Eastern Parkway subway entrance, the wheels bumping loudly as she went. The suitcase weighed as much as she did. The contents shifted suddenly, threatening to send her tumbling down the long concrete stairway. Safely at the bottom, she was immersed in a great din—the roar of trains, footsteps echoing on concrete, garbled voices on loudspeakers. She wrestled the suitcase past the crowd and through the special gate for people with strollers or large packages that wouldn't fit through the turnstile, and then down the long ramp and onto the platform for the Number 2, headed farther downtown in Brooklyn and then under the East River to Manhattan. When a train pulled in a few moments later, the car was packed with commuters on their way home from work, but several passengers stepped back from the door to make room for Carolyn and her luggage.

As the doors started to close, Carolyn was startled when she turned to see two police officers with a formidable-looking German shepherd come into the car. Her palms began to sweat despite the cold, causing her hands to slip momentarily from the suitcase's handle. It wasn't unusual for the police to make a quick scan of a subway car before stepping back off, but this time they stayed on.

The train rumbled out of the station. The officers began looking around, talking to each other. The train made one stop, then headed out again.

The officers walked to the far end of the car, then turned and headed back toward Carolyn. The shepherd was staring at her suitcase, one of the officers holding the dog as it strained against its leash, its nose down, its tail straight out. The dog began to whine.

"Oh, my God," Carolyn said to no one in particular.

"Miss," said one of the officers, a beefy young man in a standard-issue dark blue NYPD jacket, one thick hand on the dog's collar. The train pulled into the next station and the doors opened. "Would you please step out of the car?"

Carolyn had known Gracie was dead as soon as she had opened the gray metal apartment door. If Gracie were still alive, she would have been at the door, tail going like a rotor blade, barking and squirming with joy. Every now and then, she would greet Carolyn with the leash in her mouth, her eyes closed in that familiar golden retriever grin that said, *Let's walk!* Carolyn would drop her shoulder bag and briefcase, and head back out the door with her.

The afternoon light had been streaming through the soot-stained window, the subway grumbling far below the cramped two-room apartment. Carolyn could see her beloved dog—the graying snout, the honey blond body—curled up, as if sleeping, on her blue Orvis bed, a Christmas gift from her devoted owner two years earlier.

Though she had been expecting it, Carolyn was still paralyzed by the wrenching tableau. She had never loved anything, or anyone, the way she had loved that dog. Nor had anything ever loved her that much.

She looked around the small apartment, already a different space, like some kind of still life. The sounds outside seemed more distinct now—sirens, horns, truck engines, clanging pipes, coughing, a TV show seeping through the thin walls. Gracie's water dish was full, kibble still in her food bowl, the day's ration of rawhide chews and peanut butter–stuffed bones untouched.

So she had died in the morning.

Gracie's balls and toys were in a circle near her bed. One was near her mouth; the yellow one, her favorite.

Gracie had always been obsessive about chasing and retrieving, her eyes wide and tail wagging as she brought each of her toys over to Carolyn and deposited them at her feet. Whether Carolyn was on her cell, online, or reading, she would pick up the toys and simply hand them back. There was no room to throw them, and, in any case, the neighbors would have complained about the noise they would have made. But it didn't matter to the dog. Gracie never tired of this ritual. When Carolyn got sick of it, she'd pick up all the toys and balls and stuff them in the closet, or else the poor dog would have run back and forth until she collapsed.

Carolyn had first encountered Gracie running loose in a vacant lot near Prospect Park. When the limping, emaciated dog trotted over with a rolled-up newspaper in her mouth, Carolyn knew all she needed to know. She and the dog had walked straight to a nearby vet, Gracie carrying the two-day-old *New York Times* all the way. The vet said she had been starved and neglected. Six-hundred-dollars-that-Carolyn-didn't-have later, Gracie was shiny, happy, and healthy. Carolyn put up Lost Dog posters in the neighborhood, but weeks went by, and nobody came to claim her.

From that first day on, they became constant companions. They rode out blizzards together, went to the beach, visited the dog run every day. When Carolyn worked at her computer, Gracie offered herself as a warm footrest. And like a proud mother, Carolyn put Gracie's photo up on her Facebook page.

Whenever Carolyn went to the corner café for coffee, Gracie sat outside and waited, never taking her eyes off the door. She had many more friends in the neighborhood than Carolyn did, and their walks were punctuated by greetings from neighbors, doormen, cops on patrol, delivery people. Gracie was just one of those dogs that made people smile. She connected Carolyn to the world in a way she had never really been able to do herself.

But Gracie had been diagnosed with congestive heart failure more than a year earlier. "It could have been something much worse," Dr. Meyer had told her, pointing to a gray shadow over the dog's ribs on the X-ray. "She's had nine years, a good life for a golden," he said. Five of those years had been with Carolyn. "She'll probably die in her sleep. There's not much we can do." The last-alternative surgery was invasive, painful, expensive, and doubtful. Carolyn had said no.

Now here she was, down on the floor, her face buried in Gracie's gray cold muzzle.

Outside, the sun had already moved past the enormous buildings across the street, and the apartment was now cloaked in the late-afternoon November gloom.

It was a long time before she got up. Carolyn remembered how Gracie got her through her mother's death, and later, Keith's walking out on their five-year relationship. Gracie was there when Carolyn got laid off, when her sister got sick, when a date went sour, when the nights got lonely. It was Gracie who kept love alive for her whenever it was like a flickering candle, always threatening to go out.

Carolyn sat quietly on the floor, stroking the dog, as it approached dinnertime. Only then did it occur to her to wonder about Gracie's body, what she would do with it. She was in the middle of Brooklyn, not on some farm upstate where dogs could be buried in the woods. She had no idea what people did with the bodies of dogs. The thought panicked her a little. She called Dr. Meyer's office. He was still there, the receptionist said, and after a few minutes, he came on the phone.

"Gracie is dead," she said, her voice unsteady but clear.

There was silence on the other end of the phone, and Carolyn thought for a second that they'd been disconnected.

The doctor sounded concerned, but also distracted. Carolyn could hear phones warbling and nervous dogs barking in the background. She wondered how many times he had to do this in a week.

"I don't know what to do now." She imagined putting

Gracie in a garbage bag and leaving her on the curb. Did people really do that?

The vet cleared his throat. "Bring her in here if you can."

Carolyn was startled.

"Do you have a large suitcase?" asked Dr. Meyer. "We'll have her cremated and return the ashes to you. There's no other way to do it in New York. No taxi will touch a dead dog. There's an animal hearse from an animal undertaker in Queens, but it costs a lot—four or five hundred dollars."

Carolyn took a deep breath. She thought of the vet bills, the special food and medicines. She had piled up nearly $1,000 on her VISA, most of it for Gracie. She couldn't do another $500. It just wasn't there. These days, Carolyn had started to feel like a character in one of O. Henry's shopgirl stories. Some weeks, she had just enough for bread and milk.

Dr. Meyer said he had an emergency, and asked her to hold for Carmen, the bossy Venezuelan woman who ran his office. Carmen had big hair and an even bigger heart. Dripping in gold jewelry, she dressed more for a nightclub than a veterinary clinic, but Gracie had adored her, in part for the biscuits she kept in jars on her desk. Carmen knew the name of every pet the clinic saw, and ruled the anteroom with an iron fist.

"Bring her here," Carmen echoed. "Get her into a suitcase and on the subway. Just look out for the transit cops. It's not illegal, really, but it's not exactly legal either. You know how they are these days with bringing things onto the trains."

Carolyn really *didn't* know how they were. She never brought anything strange onto the trains.

"I'm here till eight tonight," said Carmen, and then she was gone.

Carolyn went to the cabinet, but the garbage bags she had were too small. She left Gracie and walked two blocks to the convenience mart. They had some fifty-gallon extra-ply bags, so she bought a box of twelve.

When she got back into the apartment, she opened the package and pulled out two of the bags. She stuck one inside the other, then laid them on the floor beside the dog bed. Gracie's tongue hung out of the side of her mouth, so Carolyn gently tucked it back in. She slipped the open end of the bags over Gracie's head, pulling them across the dog's stiffening body. When they got stuck on Gracie's protruding legs, Carolyn tugged and pulled but could not seem to fit the rest of her into the bag. Her arm began to hurt, and she realized she was sweating—the two bags tore, ripped apart by Gracie's claws. Soon Carolyn had gone through the whole box of garbage bags.

"I'm so sorry," Carolyn said aloud. She went to get a pair of scissors, then used them to cut the bags open, wrapping them around Gracie, then putting tape around the whole messy package.

An hour later, it was done. Carolyn closed her eyes, took a few deep breaths. Gracie's legs were stiff, her body cold and heavy, the plastic slippery as it made whispering, crinkling sounds. Gracie had always been so soft and warm, and Carolyn found it almost unbearable to touch her now, even through the bags. Gracie didn't smell bad—at least not yet—but her smell was already different.

Carolyn laid the suitcase on the floor, opened it, and tried to wrestle the bundled dog inside. Gracie's head slipped out of the wrapping, and her legs didn't quite fit in the case. Carolyn closed her eyes and pushed the forelegs in toward the body.

She kept thinking she was hurting Gracie. She tried to be gentle.

God, she thought, I can't do this. But she had no one to ask for help.

She grabbed Gracie's legs again and bent them forward. The legs were unyielding, but finally they bent, and at last the dog was fully in the case. Carolyn zipped it, and then sat back, feeling paralyzed.

After a few moments, she stood up and struggled to stand the suitcase filled with Gracie's dead weight upright. Then she pulled on her coat and rolled the bag out of the apartment, through the hallway, into the elevator, and out into the street.

It was raining steadily as Carolyn walked down the sidewalk, the wheels of the black bag clunking heavily along the concrete. She wondered if people could sense from the way the bag moved that there was something other than clothes in it, but nobody paid much attention.

When she got to the subway stairs, she paused. She hated the thought of banging Gracie down all those concrete steps, but there was no choice. The suitcase bumped down one stair after another, and then Carolyn rolled it through the handicapped door and down to the platform. Her arm hurt, but she held the suitcase close to her and rolled it onto the train when it clamored into the station.

Once on board, Carolyn stood by the door, clinging to a pole. She was, she noticed, the only person on the crowded car with a suitcase. As the train left the station, she clutched the bag's handle protectively.

It was a few minutes later that she had noticed the big dog coming, the two officers behind it.

Carolyn had had only a few encounters with police officers in her life. She came from a family of law-abiding schoolteachers from Queens. One of the young officers seemed to sense her fear. She saw that his name was Sanchez.

Commuters backed away as she and the two officers, along with the whining German shepherd, moved out onto the platform. The officers were looking at her, curiously but not unsympathetically, and then their gazes shifted down at the bag.

"Look," Carolyn said quietly, "I've got a dead dog in there. I'm on my way to the vet."

"You're going to see a veterinarian, with a suitcase with a dead dog in it?"

Officer Sanchez bent down and felt the side of the suitcase, then quickly recoiled.

"Miss, I'm going to have to ask you to walk," the other officer said. "Or call a car service. You can't take an animal on the subway, dead or alive. Okay?"

She looked out and saw that she was only at the Bergen Street station. There were still three stops until Borough Hall, where Dr. Meyer's office was. She blinked away tears. "It's a really long way."

Officer Sanchez shook his head. The other policeman rolled his eyes up at the ceiling, a now-I've-seen-everything look.

With a sigh, Carolyn began pulling the suitcase toward the stairs and up two flights to the exit. Officer Sanchez hurried to give her a hand, heaving the suitcase up the last dozen or so steps.

"Sorry about your dog," he said, as she began the long walk down Court Street.

Carolyn pulled out her cell phone to call Carmen. "Dr. Meyer is leaving, but I'll wait for you," she said.

It was raining, a cold November drizzle made all the gloomier by the early darkness. The suitcase rolled easily, although Gracie kept shifting inside, and the bag kept tilting, especially when Carolyn had to negotiate the curbs at intersections. Gracie's last walk, she thought.

Every now and then, to the confused looks of passersby, Carolyn found herself speaking to the suitcase. On their walks, Carolyn had always liked to speculate with Gracie about the wealth, character, fame, and employment of the people they passed. "Doctor," she would say. Or "Wall Street." Or "psycho."

But now, Carolyn was tired and hungry. The cart vendor on the corner was closing up. She asked if she could still get a pretzel, and he nodded, but it was cold and stale. The rain was steady, nearly freezing. She usually shared her pretzels with Gracie, who loved to walk with a piece in her mouth, sometimes for blocks. Sometimes, she even waited to get home to eat it. Now, Carolyn tore the pretzel in two and threw one half in the trash, and began gnawing on the other.

"Hey," she whispered to the suitcase. "Academic."

A tall man with a tweed hat and goatee rushed past, a backpack bobbing from his shoulders, an oversized umbrella in his hand. "Maybe a therapist," she added.

A young dark-skinned, athletic man in sweatpants and a hooded sweatshirt jogged past them. "Derek Jeter. Not." She was always seeing hot athletes and movie stars and pointing them out to Gracie. "Not," she would always add. Except once, when Mike Judd had been walking by and stopped to fuss over Gracie, who licked his hand. Carolyn was tongue-tied, barely able to mumble Gracie's name in answer to his question.

As she waited at a crosswalk, she nearly stepped on a Pekingese on a long leash, yipping and barking at her and the suitcase.

"Rat," she said to Gracie in a voice that was unintentionally loud. The woman holding the leash glared at her, but kept on going.

Tonight, there weren't many people walking on Court Street. After "Derek Jeter," she spotted two Wall Street types, Mayor Bloomberg (not), and a serial killer, alerting Gracie to each one as she went.

After about half an hour, Carolyn felt a blister forming on her right hand from the suitcase handle. Her sneakers were sopping wet, her socks drenched. Twice, the suitcase had banged into her ankle. The first time had left a small bruise. The second time, the hard plastic corner gouged her near the Achilles tendon, sending a small trickle of blood into the back of her shoe.

When she finally got to the clinic, she opened the door and was hit by a wave of grief. Gracie's last walk. She began to cry.

"I'm sorry," she said, sobbing as Carmen came out from behind her desk and put an arm around her.

"Take off your coat, sit down. I'll take Gracie from you."

The tiny waiting room was empty, most of the lights turned off. Carmen took the suitcase and began rolling it to an office in the rear.

"Wait," Carolyn called out, and Carmen stopped so that she could kneel beside the suitcase and put her arm around the top. After a moment, she got up, watching as Carmen pulled the suitcase into the back. She wished she had thought of something appropriate to say.

"Bye, Gracie," she said, her eyes filling up.

In a few minutes, Carmen returned with the empty suitcase.

Carolyn looked up at the fliers for lost dogs and cats and the posters about rabies, ticks, and Lyme disease. She saw a leaflet titled "When You Lose Your Pet" and took it, putting it into her pocket to read later.

Carmen made some entries into the computer, and told Carolyn the cremation costs ranged from $300 to $700, and she had her choice of styles of urns.

Carolyn chose a small jar. Gracie would rest on the window ledge overlooking Eighth Street, where she had always liked to look out. It would take about three weeks for the ashes to come back, Carmen told her.

As Carolyn stood to leave, Carmen said, "Say, could you do us a favor?"

Carolyn couldn't imagine what sort of favor the clinic would want of her.

"We have a few puppies that came in Sunday and we don't have any room. You have a crate in your apartment, right?"

Gracie's old crate was in storage down in the basement, but Carolyn hesitated.

Carmen clucked reassuringly. "It would just be for a few days. There was an apartment fire on Nostrand Avenue, and a whole bunch of dogs came in here, including these puppies. Some nearly died of asphyxiation. We can't keep them all here, and so we're asking some of our clients if they can take one for a couple of days."

It seemed disloyal to bring home another dog, even for a day or so. What would Gracie think, to see another dog in the apartment, just hours after she had died?

Carmen seemed to read her mind. "No pressure, hon. But this would just be until we find a place for them. They're nine weeks old, don't even have names yet. We gave them all their shots, though."

Carmen was forging ahead, guiding Carolyn's arm, the two of them walking to the rear, past the examining rooms, the surgical suite, the crates for sick and boarding dogs. When they got to the end of the hallway, Carmen turned the knob on an aluminum door, and they entered a small, dimly lit space, not much bigger than a broom closet. There were six crates in the room, two of them holding puppies.

"We call this the Last Resort room, where the hard cases and lost causes go," she said. "Some of the techs can't even bear to come in here, since this is where the dogs and cats go when people don't pick them up or when people bring them in off the street. The fire department brought these in Sunday."

Carmen switched on the overhead light and went over to one of the crates full of squirming puppies, and opened the top, reaching in and pulling out one of the dogs.

"This one's a female, very sweet, very social. There was some coughing and vomiting from smoke, but now she's okay."

Carmen put the puppy down on the table. She was a fat little thing, with piercing eyes. She yawned, then her tail began wagging when she looked up at Carolyn, meeting her eyes. The pup scrambled toward her, and Carolyn picked her up. She was brown and black, some sort of shepherd-collie mix. She was soft and so warm. Carolyn felt her heart rising in her chest.

"I'm calling her Faith," said Carmen. "Because we have to have faith that she'll get a home."

"Or Hope," Carolyn said.

"Or Hope," Carmen agreed.

Carolyn leaned forward, almost touching noses with the puppy, who licked her face. She drank in the puppy smell, closing her eyes.

Carmen was busy tending to the other puppies. With her back to Carolyn, she said, "A lot of people come in here and tell me they can't go through it again, aren't sure they can handle losing a dog again. But lots of dogs need homes, lots of people need dogs. Life goes on, right, honey?"

Carolyn pressed the puppy's head beneath her chin. Hope licked her face, sighed, then went to sleep.

There was no way she could put the puppy into that smelly old suitcase, which she realized she would probably throw away as soon as she got home. She tucked the puppy under her coat, right below her neck, leaving room for her to breathe.

As they walked out together, Carmen wished her good luck, gave her a hug, and then locked the door behind her.

Carolyn headed for the subway with the puppy under her coat, pulling the empty suitcase behind her. At the top of the entrance, she paused. She didn't think she could endure that again. She saw a yellow cab cruising by with its lights on, so she lifted her right hand, even though cabs were for Wall Street types and tourists, in her mind. The cabbie—a young, chubby, dark-skinned man—asked if she wanted the suitcase to go in the trunk.

No, she said, but the driver got out anyway to help her get it into the backseat. "Wow, it's pretty light," he said with a smile. "Short stay, huh?"

She didn't answer, her thoughts were on the cab fare, the cremation bill, on the food she had to buy for Hope. As the cab pulled away from the curb, there was a sharp yelp from inside her coat. Carolyn looked into the mirror and saw the quizzical eyes of the young driver.

"I don't mind," he said. "Just don't let it out."

She smiled, relieved.

"New dog?" he asked. "I've got a yellow Lab. Trixie."

Carolyn had never been good with strangers, and hadn't really talked to a man her age for a while. But she started talking now. She could hardly believe the words pouring out of her mouth. She told the driver—his named was Jared—about hauling the dead dog around in a suitcase, about the cops kicking her off the subway, about meeting Hope.

Jared listened, nodding sympathetically. He turned off the meter at $4. "This trip won't be expensive," he said. "On the house."

They sat for nearly a half an hour in front of her building, discussing their dogs. Hope crawled out of Carolyn's coat, and into the front seat, right into Jared's lap while they talked.

Jared asked if he could bring Trixie to meet Hope in Prospect Park on Saturday. It would be good for her to play with a puppy. Trixie was old and sick. He would have to face losing her soon.

"Had to be rough," he said, his face full of kindness and sympathy.

"It is," Carolyn said. And she thought of Gracie, suddenly, as a kind of love that just kept giving.

"But life goes on, doesn't it?"

Yankee Dog

Lisabeth pulled into the Dunkin' Donuts parking lot promptly at 3:50 A.M. As assistant manager of the franchise's first shift, it was her responsibility to fire the place up, turn on the heat, make sure the restrooms were clean, check the microphone in the drive-thru, start the coffee machines, and get the donuts in the oven.

While scurrying from chore to chore, she liked to talk. This, she found, not only woke her up, but got everybody else going too. And the thing she always liked to talk about most was dogs.

Lisabeth defined the periods of her life by the dogs she had had. When she first started working at DD, she had a Rottweiler named Tigger, a sweet-hearted nightmare of a dog that terrorized the neighborhood and finally lost a confrontation with a garbage truck. That was a tough time for her. Her mother was sick, her husband, Frank, was out of work, and they were dead broke.

And then there was Rutabaga, a small mutt of indeterminable origins, who came to work with her during the seven years she spent on the late shift, sitting outside in her car, barking at everything and nothing until closing time at midnight. This was when her two kids were little and she was struggling to be a good mom while holding down two jobs. Rutabaga always seemed to think she was doing just fine.

She had a snapshot of Casey, her golden, up on the counter above the window where she served the early risers and commuters who came through the drive-thru. Photos of all of her dogs were up on her refrigerator at home. Casey had marked Lisabeth's move into middle age, her kids growing up, and some of the fun going out of her marriage. Frank had always been a quiet, low-key man, but in recent years he had become withdrawn, losing himself—or hiding maybe—in sports, especially the New York Yankees, whose every game he watched with almost obsessive attention. Sometimes, he forgot their anniversary or her birthday, but he always knew the standings, batting averages, and the combined ERA of the Yankee pitching staff by heart. And maybe he was jealous of all the pets. Every dog or cat that she'd brought into the house had been a pitched battle until a year ago, when her beloved Casey died of liver cancer.

Frank, a night-shift supervisor at a meatpacking warehouse, had put his foot down after $2,400 in vet bills. That was it, he said. No more dog food. No more ruined couches. No more diarrhea on his grandmother's rug. No more walks in the rain and snow. No more dog hair on his sweatshirts and pants. No more peeing on the kitchen floor. No more pretzels snatched from the TV table.

No more listening to Lisabeth coo to Casey like she once had to him when they first started dating, in what he always called the "empty years," the time before Steinbrenner, the years when the Yankees weren't in it, weren't trying.

No more dogs.

Relationships, Lisabeth told Jeannie, her dawn-at-the-drive-thru colleague, were all about the little things, the small gestures, the thoughtfulness, and occasional endearments. These days, Frank didn't do any of those things. As he was fond of pointing out, he grew up in a house where there was a hot meal waiting for him every night, and he expected the same from his wife. At least he hoped for it. But, Lisabeth said, laughing, he rarely got it. She wasn't much of a cook, and was usually working at one job or another, something he did appreciate.

God forbid, she thought, he would ever get up and make both of them a hot meal. That was not something he ever saw in his mother's house.

There was a kind of holding-the-line quality to their life. If their marriage wasn't exactly a fairy tale, it wasn't the worst either. They were nice to each other, offered sanctuary to their two kids, and managed to scrape up enough money to get to Lake George for two weeks every September.

Sometimes, during their twenty-nine years of marriage, Lisabeth's love of animals had made the difference for her, even if Frank was never interested. "They just find me," she told him, but his response was always the same: "Let them go find somebody else."

Until recently, Lisabeth had always found some way to get them in the house. But this time was different. Frank was really putting his foot down.

"So what are you going to do about a new dog?" asked Jeannie. Jeannie lived with her mother, and had four cats and two rescue dogs, and to be quite honest, she couldn't imagine a life with only people—with Frank, in particular—and no animals.

"I don't know," said Lisabeth. "Frank says no animals, no more dogs. He says we can't afford it. And he's probably right."

Jeannie looked up at the screen to see how many coffees she had to make. "No animals?" Her tone was incredulous.

Lisabeth took an order—double latte, six glazed, three apple-cranberry muffins, two medium hot coffees, light and sweet.

"Pull up to the window, please," she told the customer.

"Do you have to tell him?"

Lisabeth laughed. "Well, honey, you can't exactly sneak a beagle into the house and keep it a secret."

Lisabeth reached behind her for her sack of the donut holes, saved as occasional treats for dogs. It was an unofficial policy at DD to give a Munchkin to a dog if the owner asked. Mostly, they were given for free. Dogs everywhere were excited to see a DD.

Lisabeth thought she had heard a dog barking through the microphone. A minute later, an SUV pulled up, and the big head of Bailey, the Lab, was sticking out the rear window. Feeding the dogs was the best part of her job, she thought. There were about a dozen regulars, and Jim, the manager, liked to joke that you would have thought all of their customers were dogs. Lisabeth never laughed at that. The dogs were always happy to see her, and they didn't mumble into the intercom, rush their orders, squawk about mix-ups, prices, or the time it took to make a cup of coffee.

She turned to Jeannie. "I was on Petfinder again last night, and they got a beautiful dog, a rescue beagle with the biggest brown eyes you ever saw. He's healthy, and got his shots. His owner died of a stroke, and he was found starving in the house. Housebroken and all. A sweetie, they say."

"But Frank said 'no more dogs,'" Jeannie said, filling the coffee orders at her station next to the microphone.

"I know, I know," said Lisabeth.

Jeannie shook her head, silently grateful she didn't have a husband telling her what dogs or cats she couldn't get. She'd had two husbands in her life, and neither of them were worth a single one of her cats.

"The rescue people are coming to the mall to meet me after work."

"You don't have to go," Jeannie said, putting the lids on the coffees.

Lisabeth took two more orders, and then checked the monitors. "Yeah, and birds don't have to fly."

LISABETH AND JEANNIE PULLED into the southernmost parking lot by the Wedgewood Mall, the biggest in the county, and waited for the blue minivan coming up from North Carolina Beagle Rescue.

"There it is," Jeannie called out. Lisabeth flashed her lights, and the van swerved over to them.

Janet, the driver, introduced herself before opening the sliding door. Inside, there was considerable baying and howling. Lisabeth looked in and a beautiful beagle looked back at her, his tail thumping wildly behind him.

Janet closed the door. "They get too excited," she said. But Lisabeth knew that wasn't the real reason Janet closed the door. It was in case things didn't work out; Janet didn't want the dogs to get their hopes up.

Lisabeth didn't hesitate. "I'll take him."

Jeannie looked at her, a bit startled after listening all day to how Frank would never go for it.

Janet took out a form and asked Lisabeth a lot of questions. Did she have a fence? What kind of food did she use? Would she pledge to neuter the dog? How often was she home? What kind of training method did she use? Would she get the dog shots every year? Were there kids in the house? Old people? What did her husband think? Did he want the dog? Would she allow a representative to come and visit the dog? Would she walk him three times a day?

Lisabeth had been through this before, and mostly told the truth. Janet went through her drill, they exchanged forms, and Lisabeth handed over a $50 donation. Janet said she had four more dogs to drop off, all the way up to the Canadian border, so she gratefully accepted the coffee and donuts Lisabeth and Jeannie had brought over from DD.

After walking around to the back of the van to get the dog, Janet opened the crate and fastened a leash to his collar. The dog, about three years old, hurtled out of the van and began sniffing Lisabeth's sneakers, his tail going like an airplane propeller.

"They're nose dogs, you know," said Janet, "so they're not always the most obedient creatures. Especially if they smell something."

She said the dog's name was Owen. Mostly, his elderly owner and he had watched TV. He got along well with other dogs—she didn't know about cats—but he seemed relatively easygoing, at least for a beagle.

Lisabeth was on her knees, not listening much; she was too busy rubbing her hands along the side of Owen's head. She pulled a handful of biscuits out of her pocket, and the dog wolfed them down hungrily.

"This is going to work," she said, and the dog seemed to look at her in agreement.

LISABETH PULLED into the driveway of her small split-level. Frank's battered old Chevy pickup was in the driveway. From the car, she saw the TV lights flickering in the living room—the big flat screen she and the kids had gotten Frank last summer as the Yankees charged toward the World Series and flopped along the way. If she'd known they were going to be wiped out by the Angels, she would have gotten him a country-western CD, maybe Hank Williams. Or a DVD about Derek Jeter.

Her heart was racing a bit. Frank wasn't a bad guy, not really. And he had permitted a lot of dogs and who-knows-how-many cats over the years. But since Casey had passed, the loneliness had been cutting, something she could feel, like a big dark hole that sometimes felt as though it was becoming her life.

The beagle hopped out of the car and immediately put his nose to the ground, circling and circling, before following her to the back door. Lisabeth stopped, then headed into the garage. She began to tremble. He would never go for this; he would make her take this poor little guy right over to the county shelter on Route 50, where they would put him in a cage. If he was in a good mood, he might just let her call the rescue people and arrange to have the dog picked up. Janet had assured her that they would take the dog back if there was any trouble.

"Owen," she whispered, "just be still." He looked up at her with those mournful eyes.

She rummaged in the boxes lining the shelves of the garage, and the dog followed her, watching her pocket—a biscuit came out often enough to keep him focused.

She called Jeannie on her cell.

"Has he seen the dog yet?"

"No, but Jeannie, I'm scared. I'm just scared." She felt her eyes welling up with tears. "It isn't just the dog. I'm fifty-two years old, and I'm scared of my own husband. I hate being scared like that."

Jeannie told her she would come and get the dog if she wished, or go with her into the house, but Lisabeth said thanks, but no. She'd deal with it.

She turned off the cell phone, wiped her eyes on the sleeve of her orange DD shirt, and pulled the dog to her side. He looked at her curiously, but he was game, it seemed, if she was.

She took a deep breath and went back to rummaging through the boxes. She plucked out a Yankees neck scarf, something she and Frank had gotten on one of those give-away days at the new stadium. She tied the scarf around Owen's neck and walked into the kitchen, where she heard the familiar play-by-play coming from the living room.

She filled a bowl with water and set it down on the floor.

"Hey, honey," she yelled, "I'm home."

"Hey, babe," Frank called back. "I'll be out in a minute. Eighth inning. Chamberlain is holding the Blue Jays down. I just want to wait for Rivera."

Lisabeth smiled. Frank was not a religious man, but if he worshiped, it would be at the Church of Mariano Rivera, the Yankees' great closer. Or maybe Derek Jeter, their shortstop and team captain. Lisabeth recognized their talent, but couldn't help wishing both of them would get out of her life.

She got another bowl, and took out the bag of dog food

that she'd kept after Casey died. Owen gulped it down greedily.

Frank issued battle reports from time to time. Rivera gave up two hits. One more and the game would be tied. He needed a strikeout. "Come on, Mariano!" Frank shouted from the living room.

Lisabeth was still trembling. She tried to shake it off. *I'm a grown woman. I'm not a child. I'm not a coward.*

She leaned down and took Owen's leash off. The dog circled the kitchen twice and then made a beeline straight through the doorway and into the living room.

Lisabeth opened the refrigerator and pulled out a Bud Light. She might need it.

She heard a groan, and the announcer shout that Rivera had given up a walk. The bases were now loaded. He needed a strikeout or a double play. Shit, she thought. He'll be in a bad mood.

Then she heard it.

"What the fuck is this? Who are you? Christ, I thought we went over this!" In the kitchen, Lisabeth closed her eyes and held her breath.

Do your job, Owen.

The dog had ridden in the car with his head in her lap the whole way. She couldn't give him up now. Lord, she should have just called Frank, told him they were coming, given him some warning. She didn't have to ask, but she could have just *told* him.

She looked at the clock. Several minutes had gone by. Something was wrong. On the TV, the announcer made a comment about the hitter needing a new bat. A commercial came on.

What was happening? Why hadn't he called for her? Why wasn't there more shouting? Her cell beeped: Jeannie. She ignored it.

Holding her beer in her shaky hands, she walked quietly through the hallway and turned the corner. The game was back on now, and Mariano Rivera was winding up.

"Got 'em!" shouted the announcer. "Rivera does it again. Strikes out two in a row to end the game. The Yankees win! Thanks to Mariano Rivera and a late-inning home run by Derek Jeter!" The roar of the crowd filled the room, and Lisabeth's eyes went to the sofa.

Her jaw dropped. Frank was sitting on the left side of the couch, holding a bottle of Bud Light. Owen was sitting beside him, his Yankee scarf showing the interlocking insignia, the two of them watching the game. Frank had his hand on the scarf as if it were some kind of lucky charm.

"So," he said, "you went ahead and did it?" He was glowering at her, but his look softened when he turned to Owen, who was staring straight ahead at the TV as if there were a steak inside of it.

"They won," said Frank, his hand scratching Owen's ears. It looked like they did this every night. Owen seemed to relax, sniffing Frank's hand. Jeez, Lisabeth thought, they even sort of look alike.

"Where did he come from?" Frank asked, a question more than an accusation.

"North Carolina," she said tentatively, almost in a whisper.

There was a long pause as Frank regarded the beagle, who looked right back at him.

"He hopped up onto the sofa, and Rivera got a strikeout,

just like that," Frank said. "Then he looked at the set again, and Rivera got another strikeout. Till then, I thought the game was over."

Owen yawned, then curled up in a ball right next to Frank, and promptly fell asleep.

"What's his name?" he asked.

"Jeter," she said. "I named him Jeter."

Frank smiled, then laughed, ruffling Jeter's ears.

"Jeter. That's a good name for a dog," he said. "A scrapper. A winner."

Jeter opened his eyes and looked at him, his tail thumping against the couch.

"I'll get you some biscuits," he said, "every time we hit a home run or win."

Jeter lifted his head at the word "biscuits."

Frank scratched Jeter's head, behind his right ear. "We can watch the games together," he said.

He took the battered old Yankee cap off his head and put it on Jeter, who licked the brim, his long ears sticking out beneath the hat. He smiled at Lisabeth.

"Nice dog," he said.

Instinct Test

Patricia wished she weren't driving a silver Infiniti, much as she loved the sound system and smooth ride. This thought occurred to her as she drove past the peeling sign for Gooseberry Field Farm, down the long dirt driveway, past a long, rickety wood-and-wire fence, and the large herd of peacefully grazing sheep beyond. As she pulled into the grassy parking area behind the sprawling farmhouse, she kicked herself for not borrowing her sister's ancient Honda sedan. She saw a battered old Ford Ranger, two or three Toyota Tacomas, a couple of Jeeps, and two giant Chevy Suburbans, the flagship vehicle of the dog show, trial, and rescue crowd. They could squeeze four or five crates into those giant Suburbans, plus coolers filled with turkey necks, special foods, and bags of hot dogs, meatballs, liver bits, and other favored training treats, not to mention balls, ropes, and dog beds. Most of these vehicles had tents for shade, as well as lawn chairs and portable fencing. As she'd guessed, there were no other Infinitis, nor BMWs, Mercedes Benzes, or Cadillacs either.

A pediatrician, Patricia had given up her practice some years ago. Now her usual turf was the sidelines at her kids' soccer and lacrosse games, backyard barbecues, school plays, the local swim club with its vast pool, monthly book clubs in beautiful houses, or, sometimes, dinner at a French or Italian restaurant in town. Farms were not much in her repertoire.

She had heard about Gooseberry from her friend Donna at the agility and obedience classes she'd recently started attending with her border collie, Dave. Donna had driven her troubled Australian shepherd, Shasta, out to Gooseberry for some sheepherding lessons, but she'd barely made it to the farmhouse, she told Patricia, before Fran Gangi, the farm's owner, had come roaring across the fields in her ATV and started berating her about "useless and pretty dogs," and boomers in their Volvos and BMWs.

Donna had immediately turned her Mercedes around and gone home. "The woman is crazy," she said. "And rude."

If Patricia hadn't loved Dave so much, she wouldn't have even bothered to come out to Gooseberry, and she wouldn't be sitting here hoping this strange woman would approve of her car. She had no apologies to make for her money or her automobile. She had earned both.

PATRICIA HAD BEEN MARRIED to her husband, Paul, for twenty-five years, and they could count the number of times they had seriously fought. But ever since Dave arrived, they hadn't *stopped* fighting. Something told her it wasn't only about the dog.

Dave had been with Patricia for two months, acquired

from Northern Massachusetts Border Collie Rescue. He'd been found tied up in an old barn twenty miles west of Worcester, beaten and emaciated and blind in one eye. The farmer was fined, and the dog was taken away.

For sure, Dave was not like the golden they'd gotten for the girls when they were young. Honey chased balls, ate, and slept, and they could not remember that sweet creature causing a second's trouble. Sure, she wasn't the sharpest tool in the shed, but the girls had adored her, and she had been a huge part of their childhoods. They were all devastated when she died, just as their youngest was going off to college. Patricia always associated Honey with the kids. But Dave was her dog.

Paul couldn't comprehend why they needed a crazy border collie in their life right now, especially one that was closer to a wild animal than a dog, and who, clearly, didn't belong in suburban Massachusetts with no work to do. It wasn't fair to the dog or to them, he said. Somebody or something, he insisted, was going to get hurt.

Patricia had been thinking about Paul's remarks on the twenty-five-mile drive out to Gooseberry.

Dave didn't grasp the concept of eliminating outside. He would jump on tables, counters, and sofas. He was obsessive about things like mail coming through slots, or curtains blowing in the wind. He howled when he heard diesel engines, circled underneath airplanes, chased light reflecting through glass and off glasses and doorknobs. He jumped through windows, dumped all over the house, chewed up table legs, placemats, briefcases, shoes, computer wires. He dug under fences, or squeezed through them, and he tried to herd everything that moved, from trucks to police cars to children.

Whenever Dave heard a siren, he would tear right through a screen window or door and give chase, trying to steer the thing back toward the house. He'd almost caused a few accidents, scared a score of kids to death, and nearly triggered a half dozen lawsuit threats—none of which had materialized—from neighbors trying to protect their gardens, lawns, kids, or cats.

The last straw had been when Dave jumped right through the plate-glass window in the living room onto the lawn and took off after a sheltie that was running alongside a neighborhood jogger. Dave went to work, circling and nipping, herding both the dog and the jogger onto the front lawn before Patricia could get out there and grab him. By that time, he had nipped at the jogger's hand when he tried to push him back. And that night, still cranked, he had also nipped Paul's ankle. Harming two people in one day, one of them her husband; this was something new. The jogger said he would call the police if he ever even saw Dave again. Paul said enough was enough.

She couldn't really say he was wrong, but she also couldn't let the dog go, not without trying everything. And everybody (apart from Donna) said that Fran Gangi was the best hope for crazy working dogs at the end of their tether, damaged and aggressive border collies being her specialty. People brought her dogs from all over the country, and she was legendary for "flipping" them around, changing even the most extreme behaviors. And she was also known for hating most of the people who brought them.

Now, in the rear seat of Patricia's Infiniti, Dave was going mad at the sight of the sheep, barking, whining, bouncing off the windows that Patricia hurriedly closed most of the way. There were drool and scratch marks all over the Infiniti's leather interior.

Patricia had never seen Dave quite this excited. She had no crate to put him in. He hated crates, and she couldn't bear to stuff him into one.

She should have closed the window all the way, but Dave loved to stick his head out, and she loved to see his happy face in her rearview mirror. It was tough for her to say no to Dave, and she knew it. She hadn't had this problem with her children.

"Dave, calm down, take it easy," she hissed. "You're going to give a bad impression or go right through the window. Knock it off."

Patricia wondered what on earth she was thinking talking to a crazy dog who had never paid the slightest bit of attention to anything she said, unless it was "Frisbee" or "ball."

Patricia had to admit she felt a little silly. A doctor, a mother, a member of the town school board, and here she was driving out into the country. For what? So a messed-up border collie could meet some sheep and pass a herding test to qualify for herding lessons?

The odd thing, she knew, was that in spite of everything, she loved him to death from the second she laid eyes on him in the shelter, where he tore out of the crate and into her lap with a look that said, *Please get me outta here.*

So she had to do something. She couldn't remember too many times in her life when she had asked for help, but here she was at Gooseberry Field Farm.

"Come on out," Fran had offered on the phone. She told her that, with border collies, you had to find work for them. "Lots of people get border collies who shouldn't have them," she said. "A lot of these dogs live in the suburbs with people in fancy houses and nice cars," she added ominously.

"I signed him up for an agility class," Patricia told her, to show she was serious.

"Is he running through those hoops in agility?"

"Yes, he is."

"Well, that will make him crazy if he isn't already."

Dave had peed in Paul's closet that morning, and Paul had stepped in it rushing to get dressed before a car came to pick him up and take him on the first leg of his trip to Shanghai.

"If this trainer thing doesn't work, then the dog needs to be gone when I get back," he said. "I'm sorry, honey. He's just not the right dog for us. Somebody's going to get sued or hurt, or the house is going to get wrecked. We both have to live here, and a dog is something we both ought to feel comfortable with."

All true, she thought. And fair. She hadn't even bothered to argue.

SHE SAW SOME of the other people showing up for the herding test. Sneakers and jeans, sweats, belt pouches, and long leads. She did not belong here, that was for sure.

Across the parking area and a couple of hundred yards into the pasture was a square fenced-in area with a half dozen sheep inside, all of them looking nervously at the spot by the gate where the dogs were beginning to appear.

Patricia got a leash out of the back, clipped it onto Dave's collar, and he lurched out of the car, barking wildly in the general direction of the sheep, pulling and spinning around.

"This must be Dave," said a voice from behind her.

Patricia turned to find a tall woman with long brown hair sticking out from beneath an Australian-style slouch hat, a long outer coat hanging down nearly to her ankles, covering a heavy pair of boots and a skinny, angular frame. She was carrying a long wooden walking stick with a carved ivory sheep head at the top. Patricia had never seen anything quite like it.

"Fran Gangi," she said, offering her hand. "And you are?"

"Patricia Worthington," she said. "We talked on the phone."

Obviously she knew that, thought Patricia, if she'd figured out who Dave was. She already felt stupid.

Fran nodded, taking in the Infiniti, and then Dave, who was staring intently at her, and at the greasy pouch hanging off her belt under the coat.

"I heard you don't like fancy cars," said Patricia coolly, but with a smile. It was not in her nature to be deferential, at least not for long. But she didn't have any idea what else to say.

"You can't believe everything you hear," Fran said, seeming to appreciate Patricia's directness. She had the sense that Fran didn't give a shit about what anybody thought of her. Patricia admired that.

Fran leaned down for a closer look at Dave, who growled, circled, and then lunged toward the sheep. Fran reached into her pocket and held out some greasy, pungent thing. It reeked.

"Meatball and lamb's blood," Fran said.

Patricia was repelled. "He doesn't take many treats," she said. "I've tried them all."

Fran walked around her and waited, holding the meatball-looking thing in her hand. Dave turned, came over to her, and lunged up. She held the food higher in the air. He circled, barked, and lunged again.

"Dave!" scolded Patricia. "Bad boy!"

Fran raised her hand, not to Dave, but to Patricia.

"Be still, please. He needs communication and support. Not yelling."

Patricia could not remember the last time someone told her to be quiet. She opened, then closed, her mouth.

Dave continued to bark and jump up and down. The other dog people were all turning to watch, and Patricia felt as if a flashing blue light had been attached to her head. The people, mostly women, all seemed to know what they were doing; even the dogs knew what was going on. The owners had their forms in hand, their mud boots and windbreakers on, treats in their pouches, travel mugs filled with steaming coffee, numbers strapped to their backs, plastic bags filled with treats.

After a few minutes that seemed like so many hours, Dave finally sat still, staring at Fran's hand. She lowered the treat, and he jumped up, so she raised it above her head again.

"Dave!" Patricia scolded.

"Sssssssh!" Fran hissed at her.

More cars were pulling in, more people were getting out and watching. Patricia was beet red; she could feel it, everybody looking at her, her shiny new boots, her flashy car.

Then Dave seemed to get something, as if it occurred to him that jumping up and down wasn't going to get him this sweet-smelling thing after all.

Never taking his eye off Fran and the treat, Dave sat still. Slowly, Fran lowered her hand, an inch at a time, down to him. If he moved even slightly, she'd raised it up again.

When he had stayed still long enough for her to lower it to his nose, she let him have it. She repeated this procedure several times. By the fourth time, he remained steady, waiting for the treat. Patricia had never seen him so calm.

"I've never been able to get him to do that," she said.

"I'm sure," said Fran.

"But he did it."

Fran nodded. "Never give a dog anything for free. Ever," she said, zipping up her greasy pouch.

There were approving murmurs from the women clustered around with their border collies, Aussies, shelties, German shepherds, Rottweilers, and mutts.

Fran asked Patricia if she knew what a herding-instinct test was, and she said, "Not really."

"It tests the dog's interest in sheep, in working with them. If a border collie can work with sheep, then I can help you. Because border collies will do anything to work, and once you know they want that, then you can begin to communicate with them. Getting them to calm down and pay attention to you is what it's all about."

Fran gave Patricia a form and asked that she fill it out.

"We want the dog to show sustained interest in sheep for up to three minutes. We see if you have any control over him, whether or not he uses his eyes"—she moved over to look at Dave again—"seems like this guy only has one good one, right?"

Patricia was amazed. She couldn't remember which eye was blind herself sometimes.

"We see whether he wears, runs wide, herds, or just attacks. Then we decide if we go from here."

Fran handed Patricia a pen, told her to read the form, and write a check for $125, and then get in line. "We take

VISA," she said with a smile. There was a remote credit-card machine out by the herding-instinct pen.

"Everybody who comes here thinks their dog is a working dog," she said. "Once in a while, they're right."

She looked at Patricia, then at the Infiniti.

"I don't really care what kind of car people drive, you know. It isn't any of my business. I have found over the years that some people don't want to do this work. Walk in the mud, step in sheep shit, run back and forth after their dog for weeks or months in the sun, in the rain, with flies and ticks. Some people do want to do it. And I never really know who is who. Generally, people who drive BMWs don't want to do that work, so I don't like to waste anybody's time and give false hope to any dog. You can't do what I do and like people a lot. Most people are selfish and lazy when it comes to dogs. They want their dogs to be cute little babies, and when you see how they mess them up, why would you like them? It's always the people's fault when a beautiful dog like this gets fucked up."

With that, Fran turned to walk toward the pasture.

ONE OF THE WOMEN came up to Patricia and introduced herself as Jess, as she collected her check and her form. She said she worked as Fran's assistant in exchange for free herding lessons. Her "girl, Tara," was in the car, she said, and it took Patricia a second to realize she was talking about a dog. She and Tara had been coming to Fran for two years.

Jess checked over Patricia's forms.

"Lots of us have barter arrangements with Fran because we can't afford the lessons. Fran doesn't turn anybody away for money. Some of us clean up, move the sheep, haul hay, help train, take care of the farm. But we also need people around here who can afford to pay. Keeps things in balance."

Well, thought Patricia, that was clear enough.

Jess explained that she and Dave would be given a number—theirs was 23. Jess would pin it to Patricia's back, and use an elastic strap to put it around Dave's back so Fran could see it. When it was Patricia and Dave's turn, Fran would ask them to walk around the pen two or three times so she could see how Dave acted around sheep, and then she would either ask Patricia to leave the testing area with Dave or to unleash him and see what he did.

It was important, Jess said, for Patricia to be quiet and not shout at the dog. That would only make him more confused and excited. Just take the leash off and walk around the pen. Once in a while, when Fran tells you, stop and see how the dog reacts to where you are. Two or three times, she'll tell you to turn around, and see what the dog does, whether he runs off or notices.

Patricia did not have a good feeling about this. She couldn't even get Dave to sit down in the house, or stop jumping through windows. How would he react around sheep in an open pasture?

Patricia got into line. Up ahead, she watched an Australian shepherd walk around the small corral as the sheep backed up and hunched together. The dog barked, then circled, then barked again. After a few minutes, Fran, who was standing behind a table at one corner of the test area, shouted for the woman to unleash the dog. She did, and he circled the pen steadily for nearly five minutes.

Patricia noted the dog's focus, his intensity, and his calm, qualities Dave did not possess. When the woman called him, he lay down until she came over and put the leash back on him. She had never gotten Dave to do that. It was clear that Patricia was far out of her league here.

The next dog, a German-shepherd mix, pulled his lead out of his owner's hand, lunged over the fence, and grabbed one of the ewes by the leg, dragging her around the tiny ring. Everyone froze. The ewe was bleating piteously, terrified.

The woman shouted frantically for the dog to get off, along with a number of people in line. Other dogs barked, the sheep panicked.

Fran Gangi got up out of her chair, vaulted the fence, and, using a shepherd's crook, hooked the dog around the collar and pulled him off the ewe, who was bleeding, although not seriously.

The line had practically disintegrated as the crowd gathered around the fence to see what was happening. Jess asked that everyone get back into their places.

"Oh, my God!" shouted the woman. "Zeus, bad dog! Bad dog!" Patricia thought she was hysterical at the sight of the sheep, lying still in shock, and her dog, who had wool streaming out of his teeth. Fran had tied the dog to the gate, and now she turned around and glowered at the screaming woman. "Will you just be quiet?"

Patricia expected Fran to kick the dog and its owner out of the test, but she didn't. Instead, one of the women who worked at the farm handed Fran a tube, and she turned the ewe's head, held her down, and applied an antibiotic ointment to the leg.

Patricia was struck by how calm Fran was. People got back into line. The dog seemed to settle. The injured ewe got up and jumped back into the small flock. She and the other sheep munched on some hay that had been thrown in by one of Fran's helpers.

"A few bite marks," she said. "She'll be fine. Susie, make a note of the ewe's number, will you? Number 165. We'll check on her later and we'll get her out early."

Fran asked Zeus's owner to come up to the fence and stand beside her. She walked over to Zeus, and tossed him a treat, which he refused to eat at first.

"He's still cranked up," she said. Then she threw another. And another. Finally, Zeus began eating them. He seemed to calm, to turn away from the sheep. After a few minutes, Fran bent down and untied him from the gate. Zeus looked at the sheep, then at her. She stood back a few feet, held up a treat, and then told Zeus, "Here." He walked over to her, just a few feet from the sheep, and lay down. She held him in that position for several minutes, tossing treats down around the ground. Zeus ate the treats, but never took his eyes off the sheep for long.

"You can tell he's not a border collie," Fran said quietly. "They wouldn't take the treats. Interesting."

She told the woman to leash up Zeus and take him out. "He passed," she said, filling out the form. "He's plenty interested in sheep, but we have some calming work to do first. I put him down for a retest. Talk to me later."

This wasn't like the obedience class they gave at the Y.

Fran turned to the people in line.

"This dog didn't do anything wrong," she said. "He's just doing what dogs do. The owner had no control over him, so when he got excited by the sheep, he wasn't listening. I don't know if any of you noticed, but this dog doesn't know his name. He thinks his name is 'Zeus, bad dog' or 'Zeus, come here now!' He gets yelled at for doing what any dog like him would naturally do around sheep."

The wind blew across the open field. What an incongruous scene Patricia thought. Far off to the left in this small, fenced-in area the larger flock, about two hundred sheep, grazed quietly, and at this end, a line of about fifty dogs and their owners, all stood waiting. Patricia hoped nobody would talk to her. She had no idea what to say, at least nothing that wouldn't show she had no idea what she was doing.

The next five or six dogs in a row were clearly hopeless, even to her untrained eye, running in all directions, paying no attention to the sheep at all, barking obsessively, ignoring their handlers. She had no doubt Fran would flunk them, and then her.

Finally, it was Patricia's turn.

Dave's eyes were locked on the sheep. As she circled the pen with him, he walked calmly beside her, staring at the flock as if he had been hypnotized. Fran asked her to go halfway, then turn around. She made Patricia go back and forth five or six times.

The flies were swarming, and so were the mosquitoes. The smell of sheep dung was powerful. The sun was strong on her face and neck. The sound of barking dogs was grating on her nerves.

After a few minutes, Fran asked Patricia to take Dave off the lead. When she did, he bolted, circling the pen, round and round and round, rushing past her. Each time she called to him, he ignored her. She moved toward him to try to grab him, but Fran told her to be still. She found herself shouting at the dog. "Dave! Dave! Lie down right now." She clearly didn't have control of him, and a moment later, Dave lunged at one of the ewes and bit her on the nose.

Fran came out to the fence and stood watching, taking notes, filling in the evaluation form. Patricia tried to look over her shoulder but couldn't see what she was writing.

Finally, Fran moved inside the pen, stepped in front of Dave, and dropped a few treats on the ground. He rushed past them, then stopped and sniffed the air. Fran leaned over and took his lead, handing it over to Patricia. Even as he ate the treats, Dave couldn't seem to take his eyes off the sheep.

"I know it was a mess," Patricia said, "but I'm willing to learn."

Fran was scribbling on her form. "Good for you. You flunked."

She pulled another sheet out from her clipboard and motioned for the next dog to come up, then she turned and looked Patricia over a bit.

"He's just being a border collie. The problem isn't him, it's you. You've got a great dog. He needs a better human, one who is willing to do the work with him. I have no idea if that's you or not."

Patricia was not used to being talked to in this way, and she couldn't wait to get into the car and get the hell out of there. She wanted to reach over and grab Fran Gangi by the throat and shake her like a rag doll. She wanted to be home, in her nice suburban house, not in this strange and chaotic place.

"If you want to do the work someday, come to the house and we'll talk about it. In the meantime, take a walk around the farm if you'd like. If not, you can just leave. It would be cheaper."

Patricia was thoroughly humiliated. She turned and saw a long line of women with their dogs, and their numbers pinned to their shirts. She walked Dave away from the sheep to a big plastic tub of water. He climbed right in and gulped huge mouthfuls. She hadn't realized how hot and tired he must have been. She had also never seen him so calm.

He turned and looked up at her.

"Good boy," she said, leaning over to kiss him on the nose.

There was still a long line of people and dogs waiting for their tests. Patricia walked Dave out back and down a long winding path to the car. When she called for him to get in, he was reluctant and kept looking back toward the sheep. But soon she was driving down the long driveway, leaving behind a cloud of dust.

ON THE WAY HOME, Patricia stopped at a bookstore in a mall, where she bought three books. Then she stopped at an all-night grocery. That night, she spent several hours online.

The next morning, at five A.M., she got out of bed, put on her jogging outfit, got Dave, and drove to a state park ten miles from her house. As she expected, it was nearly deserted. She called Dave out of the car, then she took out a large plastic bag filled with a special brand of meatballs—ground liver, beef, and gravy—which she had stayed up till two A.M. baking the night before. She put eight or nine of them in a smaller bag and tucked them in a fanny pack she used to hold her glasses and cell phone when she jogged.

Then she began a series of drills. Lie down. Stay. Sit. Come. She used one crisp word, not several. She made eye contact, first by holding the meatballs up to her eyes so Dave would look at them.

"Dave," she said briskly, and he would snap around to

look at her. "Down!" And she would raise her hand. At the instinct test, she had noticed that the people who knew what they were doing didn't speak to their dogs nearly as much as she spoke to Dave.

She made him lie down out of sight, behind trees, on the other side of cars, with trucks and buses roaring by.

Patricia was getting wet, muddy, cold. But she was also getting clearer as she watched Dave respond, saw his flightiness and confusion change as they worked together day after day.

Remember, he's an animal, she reminded herself, not a kid. He can be trained like an animal if he isn't treated like a child. Paul thought she'd lost her mind. He complained that they never had breakfast anymore, and that she had become obsessed.

She just smiled, and he left her alone.

She went through five greasy fanny packs before she gave in and got a rubber-lined fisherman's bag. They continued to train in the cold, the rain, and the strong sun.

One hundred times a day: "Lie down."

One hundred times a day: "Come to me."

One hundred times a day: "Stay."

One hundred times a day: "Sit."

They trained in malls, near traffic, in front of firehouses and schoolyards, alongside dog playgroups, using other dogs as distractions and bait.

She did not miss a day.

Then, one autumn Saturday, she drove back to Gooseberry Field Farm. She paid her money and got her number—30. When it was her turn, Fran Gangi waved her in.

"Hey, Infiniti," she said. "I didn't think we'd see you again. Let him off the leash."

Dave circled the pen. When he was directly across from Patricia, she raised her hand, as in a salute, and then, without a word, lowered it again. Dave dropped to the ground.

Patricia could hear the murmurs from the people behind. "That dog is good. She knows what she's doing."

She released Dave and he circled around to her. She made him lie down, then stay.

Fran told her to bring him into the pen with the sheep, and she did. Dave charged toward the sheep and Patricia leaned over the fence and said calmly: "Dave, down."

He dropped to the ground. The sheep moved away, but slowly. They were not in a panic this time. "Away," she said, and he moved to the left. She turned to Fran. "I haven't worked on 'come bye' yet," and Fran nodded, scribbling notes on her test form.

Dave circled the sheep, dropped down, nipped at one of the ewes, then came back.

Fran told Patricia to come out. "He passed. You did too. Nice work. Want to come in for coffee later?"

Patricia didn't quite understand why this felt so good, but it did. She leaned over and knelt to the ground, hugging and kissing Dave. "What a good boy. I love you," she said, and at that moment, he looked beautiful, calm, and proud, as if he had been born in that spot and had done what she'd asked every day of his life.

An hour later, Patricia walked through the front door into the strange world of Gooseberry Farm. Patricia had never been in a place like it. Old overstuffed sofas and chairs lined the big living room, and cardboard boxes filled with forms were stacked up all around, as were bags of dog food, leashes, boots and rain gear, flashlights and harnesses, balls and dog toys.

Along the walls were dozens of framed photographs of dogs, and scores of trial ribbons, agility awards, and AKC and other herding certificates.

A sofa growled at her as she went past, and only then did she realize that there were crates everywhere, dogs in almost all of them. Fran's dogs were either working or else kept in crates, to help keep them focused. They were not pets in the sense that Patricia knew the term.

She heard talking from the rear of the room, which opened up into a big kitchen. She walked over and saw Fran seated at one end of a table, logbooks and evaluation forms scattered in front of her. Five or six other women were gathered around the table, and in the middle were steaming coffee mugs, a rasher of bacon, and a tray piled with mostly burnt corn muffins.

Five of the women had dogs tethered to their chairs—two Aussies, three border collies. Patricia had put Dave in the car and left him there. She sat down, and the women all introduced themselves. Patricia had already gathered that time with sheep was precious to these women, and if they couldn't pay for the time, they happily worked their asses off hauling hay and doing farm chores in exchange. These women were completely at home in Fran's kitchen.

One woman, who introduced herself as Lisa, said, "We're here at least once a week. We all know how to eat Fran's muffins, something that should be done very carefully."

The other women laughed, and Patricia could sense how comfortable they were with one another, how at ease. It was strange, but she felt accepted in that kitchen, even though she had no reason to feel this way.

The talk was all dogs. About their encounters with other dogs, their training successes and failures, Internet hysterias about dog food, stories of dog bites and fights. About getting their dogs to listen to them, about the sweet feeling of working with a dog, of taking sheep out to pasture. About the trials they were entering, the ribbons they were seeking.

Patricia didn't say much until Fran asked her about her life and work. Patricia told them she'd given up her pediatric-medicine practice a few years ago, the liability insurance so expensive, the paperwork staggering, the fights with the health-insurance companies so relentless. Plus, she had wanted to be there for her girls, to be at home, and drive them to school, and know what was going on in their lives. She was surprised to find herself starting to choke up, and she blinked back the tears. This was no place to cry.

When Patricia said she was a doctor, Fran had perked up. They needed a medical person at the trials and instinct tests, she said. People were always getting stung, falling down, spraining their ankles, getting bitten by dogs, cutting themselves on knives and fences, falling off ATVs, even blowing out their knees. Maybe Patricia could work some of the trials as the on-duty medical person in exchange for lessons.

Patricia said yes right away, a bit startled by how quickly she'd responded. She had turned down a dozen offers to join medical practices, and yet she jumped at this. But it felt natural, comfortable, and she was suddenly eager to use her skills, to have a role to play.

It was beginning to get late, and one by one, the women got up, said good-bye, collected their dogs, and left. Patricia was a bit startled to find herself still there. When everybody was gone, Fran brought her a cup of coffee. She leaned back, shoved some of her paperwork aside, and sipped from her mug. She looked tired, Patricia thought. It was time to go. She started rise.

"About your dog," said Fran.

Patricia eased back down into the chair. In the farmhouse, she could hear the groans, sighs, and stirrings of the dogs in crates.

"How many dogs do you have?" she asked Fran, who thought about it for a minute.

"I think twelve," she said, then leaned forward. "So what's the story?" she asked. "Everybody who comes here has a story. A reason to be here. Husband issues?"

Patricia flushed, then smiled.

"I've been divorced twice," Fran said. "Both nice guys. But I mean, come on, who could be married to me and live with twelve dogs? Sorry for asking, but a lot of the women here—well, you don't see many husbands, and that's because there aren't that many. I don't know if there's a connection or not." She laughed and Patricia laughed too. Paul certainly wouldn't want to live with twelve dogs. He could do without any, really.

"No, it's the dog that got me out here. The dog was driving us crazy. Driving Paul crazy."

Fran nodded. "They were meant to work, and without work, they don't really know how to live. They get crazy and they make people crazy. Out here, they get sane. They find themselves."

Patricia had an odd feeling, as if she were at some gate and about to pass through it. She liked these women, these people. They were different. But they were real, down to earth, passionate. She had the sense that loyalty was a big thing here, and there was something loving about them too, something dependable.

"Let's take your dog out to herd some sheep," Fran said. She reached up into the closet and grabbed a flask of brandy, then put on her safari hat and cape. "You have a couple of hours?"

Fran tossed her a long leather leash that wrapped around a person's shoulder. "A shepherd's leash," she said. "You can have the dog on it, and keep your hands free."

Patricia clipped it on over her shoulders and around her waist, a seven-foot leather leash that hung from the side. Fran opened one of the crates and Sam, one of her older border collies, zoomed out. Then she handed Patricia a can of bug spray and a flashlight.

They walked out of the farmhouse together and over to the pasture gate, Patricia stopping along the way to get Dave from the car and attach the leash to his collar.

The sheep—there were more than a hundred—saw the dogs and began to gather in a block and move away. Fran opened the gate. She told Sam to stay, and he did, ears up, waiting. She looked over at Dave.

"Let him go," Fran said. "Sam is here for backup. He knows the drill. Trust him. You know, at the heart of it, the dog and the sheep know what to do. Sometimes we just have to remind the dogs we're part of it."

Fran turned to Sam, and said, "Get out there," and he tore off and ran wide and to the left of the sheep.

Patricia leaned over and patted Dave. "Be good," she said, and she unclipped the leather lead. Dave looked up at her, as if he could hardly believe it, and then took off. At first, the sheep started to run, but Dave ran wide of them and got behind them. Fran yelled at Sam to come bye, and he came over to the right of the sheep, so they had nowhere to go but toward Fran and Patricia. They came rushing through the gate, Dave on one side, Sam on the other.

Fran said, "We're bracing them. They can't really go anywhere but straight ahead."

The sheep, flanked by the two border collies, picked up steam and ran out behind the farmhouse and down a path through some woods—the two women walking rapidly behind—and then into a vast, open unfenced pasture on the far side of the house.

Fran whistled and Sam dropped down, almost vanishing into the grass.

She looked at Patricia. The sun was setting, the hills and pasture shrouded in mist. There was a rich smell of manure and fresh grass.

"Our ancestors did it," Fran said. "There's nobody in human history that didn't herd sheep with dogs at one point or another. Except maybe the Eskimos."

The wind rustled the grass, and there was a chill in the air. Dave walked steadily along the flank of the flock, watching the sheep closely. Patricia was struck by how calm he was.

"It isn't him who's calmed down, it's you," Fran offered. "The dog is just a mirror. He reads you. You've trained him and so you've set him free from all the craziness we put into their lives. People don't get that. It isn't them; it's us."

Then she looked out at the sheep. "They're trying to settle," Fran said. "When the sheep settle, the dog calms down if they're any good. It's where the dog and sheep both want to be. That's their natural position. The sheep grazing, the dog keeping an eye on things." Sam lay still, watching, as if he were teaching Dave, who was moving, but slowly, with authority.

"Tell him to lie down."

Patricia looked up and shouted, a bit louder than she had meant: "Dave. Down!" Dave slowed, turned and looked at her, as if he didn't quite believe it.

"Easy," said Fran softly. "Convince him you know what you're doing. Pretend."

Patricia raised her hand, and then dropped it. "Down," she said, so quietly she couldn't imagine that he'd heard it.

But although he was at least a hundred yards away, Dave dropped to the ground. The sheep slowed, and then lowered their heads. They spread out and began grazing. It seemed as if they had been waiting for this to happen all along. The reddish sun dropped below the hills behind the sheep, and Patricia almost wanted to cry; it was the most beautiful thing she had ever seen.

She called out to Dave, and to her surprise, he came running over to her, touched his nose against her knee, then turned and ran back behind the sheep.

She looked over to Fran, who was watching the sheep, nodding.

How wonderful and strange, Patricia thought to herself. Almost beyond understanding.

That this is my world. And I have found it.

Old Dogs

JAMES AND KIPPER ROUNDED THE HILL AT THE TOP OF THE pasture—it was little used now, and overgrown with weeds and scrub—to make their daily check on the farm's boundaries and fences. The two of them would have made a lovely pastoral painting, the still-handsome, blue-eyed, tall, and craggy old farmer with his white shock of windswept hair, and the intense and purposeful low-to-the-ground black-and-white border collie, moving rapidly but off kilter on his three legs.

James and Kipper had been patrolling the farm and its sheep and cows for many years now, twice a day, rain or shine. There was little to patrol these days, just a dozen sheep, mostly older ones James couldn't bear to send off to market.

Kipper knew every inch of the farm, and if there was so much as a new piece of paper blown by the wind, he would go to it, sniff it, mark it. The industrious dog was better than any land surveyor, thought James.

It was Kipper who alerted him now that something was wrong. His ears went back on his head, which he lowered almost level to the ground, dropping into a quiet crouch. He let out a low growl, and the fur on his back stood straight up.

James scanned the trees and bushes in front of him. His eyes were not what they used to be. He reached into his pocket and put his spectacles on. He saw nothing.

He turned and looked at Kipper, following the old dog's nose straight toward a tangle of old fence posts and barbed wire. Then he saw it.

"Hold it, Kipper," he said. "Steady there. Be careful." He took a step forward, a small one.

THERE WAS A TIME when James could stalk right up the hill without taking a deep breath, but now it took more determination. He paused two or three times on the way up, and Kipper paused with him, sitting or lying down when he stopped. He didn't know if this was a courtesy, or if Kipper was tired too. After all, he was twelve now.

"Old dogs," James liked to whisper, "two old dogs."

The walks were still magic. The smell of the barns, the hay, the flowers, and air, the manure, flitting shadows, the soil, the grip of the wind, the powerful formations of clouds steaming by, the spectacle of the sun fighting through and streaming across the valley.

He could have gone to Florida, like the other farmers, or moved into town, into one of those little ugly split-levels that were built, unlike farms, to be maintenance free. Or he could've gone to North Carolina, or into one of those assisted-care places where you gave them all your money and you took a bus to the market and doctor's appointments.

But he would truly rather be dead than to be in an ugly little house, or dependent on so many other people. And what would he do in retirement? There seemed to him nothing to do in that situation but die. How many stories had he heard of the old farmers who sold off their land, went off to trailers and condos, and were dead within weeks and months? A man had to have a purpose, had to have something meaningful to do.

And there was Kipper to think of.

He and Kipper were like extensions of each other; each reacted to the other's thoughts, read the other's mind, worked together in a seamless ballet.

Still, James had always expected that he and Helen would be facing old age together, and it had never crossed his mind that she would leave him like that, so quickly, so completely. Helen had been a farmwife, just as he was a farmer. She took care of the house, he took care of everything else, and the two of them had worked hard decade after decade, side by side.

So now it was just him and Kipper, and if Kipper left, then maybe it would be time to sell the farm and go live somewhere else. He would think about that when the time came.

In the mornings, when he and Kipper took to the fences, he heard a thousand ghosts from the past, and he wondered if the dog did too. Cows, steers, dairy and beef, goats, five hundred sheep. Potatoes and corn, alfalfa and grain. Once, he had two helpers, and it took the three of them a full day just to get the animals moved, watered, tended, and fed, to keep water troughs up, to move the manure, run the tractor, fix the fences, patch the barn. There was never enough time.

Now, it took him and Kipper but a half hour to walk the pasture, and then they were done for the day. And the only sounds were the lonely cries of the sheep, the wind, and the distant sounds of trucks whining along faraway highways.

About twenty-five yards ahead of him, he saw what Kipper had seen, and he froze. It was a beautiful, awful thing—a huge coyote caught in the barbed wire and woodpile that James had dumped there. This coyote was different than some of the scrawny ones he had seen over the years. He was enormous, his ruff thick. His eyes were large, intense, almost fluorescent. Those piercing gray eyes stared coolly right into his.

James saw the animal had struggled—he was bloody all over. But he was no longer fighting now. He was either resigned to his fate or else completely exhausted. He showed no fear, no desire to run. He didn't bare his teeth or growl.

As he looked closer, James saw a trickle of blood coming from one of his nostrils. He had been in the wire a long time. This, James thought, might be the one picking off his sheep. He had seen those tracks, and they were large.

James could tell the coyote was old. He could see it in his eyes and in his white muzzle. He had a quiet dignity about him—James had seen so many animals panic, but this one seemed poised, ready for whatever might come.

James couldn't leave this creature to die like that in the wire. He couldn't let him walk away or escape, either, to kill his sheep, or the animals of some other farmer. The rules were clear.

"Let's go back, Kipper. We have to get the rifle."

Kipper would be no match for this coyote if things went wrong and the animal got loose. Border collies were workers, not fighters. The fact that Kip had only three legs didn't seem to slow him down at all. He had worked every day of his life, including the day when he mistook Peter Elmer's tractor coming down the hill for a sheep and tried to herd it into the pasture, where he thought it belonged. It was his first failure as a working dog, and it cost him a leg, chewed up in the mower blades. After that, there had been some awkward moments with the sheep, when Kipper couldn't quite pivot and turn like he used to, but he quickly recovered, and he was still smarter and faster than any of the dozen or so Tunis sheep that James still kept on the farm. But James had seen Kipper nearly get killed countless times—kicked by donkeys and cows, tangled in barbed wire, chasing after trucks and tractors, butted by rams and sheep. He had no doubt the dog would throw himself into the coyote's jaws if it went after James or threatened the farm or the sheep.

James called sharply to the dog and began to head back to the farmhouse. Kipper kept turning around, then moving reluctantly down the hill, keeping himself between the coyote and James at all times.

Before the farm wound down, James had lost a lot of sheep to coyotes, and he was always trying to figure out what to do about it. He never quite had.

He could electrify the fence, which was expensive. But

James was no longer making any money from the farm. The old farmhouse was in urgent need of repairs to the roof and the plumbing, and the big barn was about to fall over into the road.

James hated coming out of the farmhouse in the morning and finding eviscerated carcasses scattered by the barn. In the old days, he would have sat out with a rifle and a big electric torch and picked off a couple of the coyotes. Or Kipper would have heard them coming and run them off. But Kipper, like James, didn't hear as well anymore and didn't move as fast. Nor did James want to put him at risk. The last carcass he wanted to find out on the hillside one morning was Kipper's.

James wanted to tell Helen about the coyote trapped up in the wire. She had been dead nearly three years, but he still expected to find her standing in the kitchen somehow, his coffee and toast hot and ready, after his morning walk with Kipper.

He knew Helen would feel sympathy for the coyote—she didn't take to hunters much—and say, "He's just doing his work like you're doing yours." He knew she wouldn't like the idea of his going up there to shoot him. She was nervous around guns.

But he was a farmer, and if something was threatening the farm, the farm came first.

James walked into the kitchen, Kipper alongside, and looked at Helen's apron, still hanging on its hook. He couldn't bear to take it down. Kipper jumped up onto the sofa and looked out the window, up into the pasture, where the coyote lay.

James touched Helen's apron, remembering her last days, her last words, as she gripped his arm. "Oh, Luke," she said, calling out to their lost son, his life given for his country in a war James didn't understand. "Oh, Luke."

James always imagined that Helen had never quite forgiven him for Luke. James and the boy had never really connected. Luke grew up angry, resenting the farm, as if it had taken something from him. He never wanted a farming life, wanted to get away as soon as possible. Helen always said James was more patient with the animals than with his own son.

Luke had had a rough time as a teenager—drinking, fights, trouble in school. When he was arrested for shoplifting at a local department store, James told him he needed to go into the Army, because he thought it would be good for him. In James's time, the Army was thought to build character. Somehow he missed that the world had changed. He didn't see it until it was too late. Luke was killed in a helicopter crash in Vietnam, and Helen was never really the same. When she talked about the old men who sent the young ones off to die, he always felt she was talking about him.

James had never mentioned Luke after the funeral, not to Helen, not to anybody. Once a year, they went to the cemetery together, and he held her hand while she cried.

Then they found those lumps in her chest, and she was dead six months later.

Kipper was his only consolation, the only creature in the world, he thought, that he had never disappointed, and who always—always—would rather be with him than with anyone else.

JAMES SHOOK OFF HIS MELANCHOLY. He had a job to do. He went into the back closet and took out his old .30-06, his deer gun.

One quick round in the head ought to do it. Then the old bastard would not bother anybody's sheep anymore. Though he was a beautiful animal, he had to admit that. He told Kipper to stay in the house—the dog was whining and rushing at the door, but he pulled it shut.

James checked the cartridges, slid one in, pulled the breech, checked the safety. He would get as close as he could, try to put one between the eyes, as he had done for rabid raccoons, wounded deer hit by cars, even a sick stray dog or two. Up here on the farm, this is what you did.

James's legs throbbed, and he was sweating through his chamois shirt. The morning had started out cool, but the sun was strong now. Kipper, outraged to be left behind, was barking and protesting loudly from the house.

James opened the pasture gate and made his way up the hill, about a thousand yards on a gentle slope. He held the rifle safely, pointed down to the ground, but he had the safety off. He needed to be ready to shoot. He hoped he could shoot straight. It had been a few years since he had used the rifle, and his hands were not so steady.

At the top, behind a stand of pine trees, was the pile of wire and posts where the coyote had gotten himself snagged. James turned the corner and was startled to see that the coyote was closer to him than he expected, maybe five feet. Somehow, he'd thought he was farther back in the woods.

The coyote turned to him, looked calmly in his eyes, then looked down the hill. God, thought James, he was a sight, a regal thing. Especially up close. He had the most powerful eyes.

He knew what the coyote was looking at even before he heard the barking. Kipper was tearing up the hill, head down, ears back. James hadn't checked the front windows, he'd probably left one open. For that matter, he wouldn't be surprised if the damned dog had gotten hold of some tools and unscrewed the hinges on the back door.

"Foolish dog," said James as Kipper hopped up and stood beside him, giving the coyote a cold stare.

Kipper positioned himself between James and the coyote and lay down. The coyote met the dog's stare, and James marveled again at how cool this creature was, how dignified, as if he were waiting for this, expecting it, not surprised at all to be confronted with an old farmer and his old dog. The dog, too, surprised him. He was calm, almost quiet, not frantic, or barking loudly, or even growling.

The three old dogs looked at one another.

The coyote raised his head, and James could see more blood caked on his neck. How he must have suffered, lying in that tangle. It reminded him of all those awful pictures of Jesus coming down off the cross.

Kipper was as still as James had ever seen him. By his position the dog seemed to say to the coyote, *As long as you stay away from him, I have no quarrel with you. But I will not move away from him, and you will have to go through me to get him.*

The coyote was lying on his side, his legs tangled in wire and his back and side resting on some bushes and posts. His stomach was moving up and down slowly. He lowered his head to rest on the top of a cracked old fence post, but he never took his eyes off James.

James held up the rifle, and the wind whistled up the hill and blew leaves among the three of them. He hoisted the gun up under his right arm, the butt on his shoulder, and took a step forward. He had the coyote's forehead right in his sights. He could hardly miss.

But something held him there.

He lowered his rifle and he looked down at the farm that he loved so much, and that his father had loved so much, and his grandfather, and great-grandfather before him. At the handful of grazing sheep still there—soon to leave—and the rotting old barn and fading farmhouse and busted engines and cannibalized old trucks.

Then he raised the rifle again and sighted it on the coyote.

"What is it that happens to life?" he said out loud, to Kipper, "that it slips by so fast, and that we don't see it go? What happened to my boy and my Helen? It was only yesterday that the three of us picnicked right here up on this hill, brought cheese sandwiches and fresh cider and we ate it right here."

The wind came up again, and he heard Kipper whine and stir.

And through the gun sights, he swore he saw tears running from the beautiful creature's big yellow-gray eyes, streaming down the side of his long gray pointed nose. He saw shadows on the ground, and he heard the leaves and grass rolling and rustling in the wind, and he looked back up at the big birds, already waiting to pick the wounded animal apart. They could smell blood a long ways off.

Then James felt hot tears running down his own face too. He raised his arm and wiped his eyes on his old flannel sleeve.

He pulled the trigger, and a cloud of birds lifted up right over his head; the sheep bolted and ran toward the shelter of the pole barn, and Kipper shivered.

James heard the sound of the shot reverberate and bounce off trees all through the valley, and he wondered if somebody would look up and come see. But he knew they wouldn't. It wasn't an unusual thing around here, to hear a shot like that.

He lowered the rifle. He was done.

HE WONDERED LATER if he had moved his arm deliberately, or if he just wasn't used to the gun anymore. He had shot high, tearing a huge chunk of bark off a nearby maple tree.

The coyote never flinched. His eyes were still locked on James. James felt light-headed, almost dizzy. The coyote's eyes seemed to blaze, then blur. He heard the whispers: *Oh, Luke. Oh, Luke.*

James heard himself sobbing, short, deep gutteral cries, more animal-like than human. He hadn't cried when Luke died. He hadn't cried when Helen died. But he cried now, as if his grief were rising from a new well that had been dug up inside him, great piercing sobs that rolled across the pasture.

James dropped the gun. Kipper stepped ahead of him, and then James, all of the fear and hesitation gone, walked right up to where the coyote lay. He reached into his pocket and pulled out the cutter he always carried for the fences and began clipping the barbed wire away.

The coyote lay quietly panting, watching as, bit by bit, the cutters snipped until he was finally free. He rolled backward and down to the ground.

Kipper growled, and leaned forward. The coyote turned and locked his eyes on to Kipper, and for a second James thought his heart would explode right out of his chest.

He started to look for the gun where he'd dropped it, and then he stopped. James stepped back and called Kipper. Kipper sat down and waited, a few feet alongside of him, refusing the command to get back.

After a moment, the coyote struggled to his feet, shook his head as if to clear it. Then he turned, and looked at James, right in the eye. The strangest thing, he thought. He felt a shiver down his spine.

And the coyote was gone.

JAMES HAD A LONG DREAM about the coyote that night. He saw him looking up at the sky, rolling over, and lying still. He saw his eyes, still blazing in the moonlight. There was something powerful about them, almost radiant.

The next morning, James and Kipper came out for their morning chores. Up near the pasture, they saw the crows and buzzards circling at the top near the gate. James grabbed a shovel, and he and Kipper took a long walk up. It was a warmer day, less windy. The shovel was heavy by the time they got up to the mound of wire and fence posts.

They saw the birds under a pine tree fifty yards away, on the edge of the deep woods. The buzzards took off, complaining as Kipper and James came near. There, curled up under the tree, was the body of the coyote.

James took a swig from the thermos he had filled with ice water, and then he started to dig. He had to rest two or three times, and his blue work shirt became soaked with sweat. His hands blistered until they turned bloody. His boots chafed his feet, rubbing the skin raw. His knees and elbows throbbed in agony. But he kept digging, the mounds of soil growing along the sides of the trench. By noon, he had a hole dug deep enough to keep other predators out.

He crossed himself and said a silent prayer, and then, using the butt end of the shovel, he pushed the coyote into the grave, covered it with dirt and moss, and then carried a dozen rocks and boulders over to put on top of it. The old coyote would have some dignity. Kipper lay alongside him all morning.

"Old dog," James said, "rest in peace."

He and Kipper walked down the hill, side by side, and then into the farmhouse, where James gave Kipper some fresh water and made some iced tea for himself.

He glanced over at a photograph of Helen, a portrait sitting on the table. He looked out the window, at the handful of sheep up on the hill. He gazed down at Kipper, who was staring at him intently, perhaps because James didn't often sit quietly like this.

Kipper was ready and eager for work, whatever it was, whatever was next.

To the dog, James said, "Kipper, I think we can't be living like this anymore."

To himself, he wondered what life off the farm might be like. He wondered if there could be another kind of life. Could there be fun? Warmth and comfort? An easier life for him, and for Kipper? A smaller place? Might there be another companion for him, someone to share life with him and Kipper in the time left?

Somebody from the community college over in Argyle had asked him if he might teach a noncredit course in farming and hay management for the kids there. His hay was legendary around the county for its nourishing quality, its long life. They had a small stipend—$1,000—that they could pay him.

He had said no, but now, he wondered if he might not like it. And they were looking for a judge at the county fair, for the cows and the sheep. He would enjoy that too, putting to good use what he knew, working with kids.

And somebody had called and offered to pay him to do some sheepherding demonstrations at the new organic sheep-cheese farm down the road. Kipper would like that, and there were lots of other festivals and fairs that might be interested too. And he knew people would love to watch a three-legged herding dog. James had always said no, he was too busy, he didn't have time. But now, maybe he did.

He was not into mystical mumbo-jumbo, but he couldn't get the coyote out of his head, or shake the feeling that the coyote had come for him, not his sheep. He kept seeing his eyes, the way he ended his life. It had shaken him, opened him up.

He looked back over at Helen, a bit guilty maybe, thinking about a companion, but he knew what she would say because she had said it to him a few days before she died: "James, don't die a grumpy old farmer. Be happy. You've suffered enough. Have some dreams. Take care of Kipper." He felt his eyes well up. He got out his handkerchief to wipe them dry.

He looked back over to the photo. "I'm sorry, Helen. I wish I'd been a better husband, a better father. Sometimes, it feels like the farm just ate me up. Like life ate me up. But I still have some time." The dog whined, and came over to him. Kipper looked confused, perhaps anxious, caught up in the tone of James's voice.

"See what happens when you lie around, Kip?" he asked the dog, who looked at him curiously, tilting his head.

Then, James leafed through the phone book and made a call.

"Harriett?" he said. "You remember me? James Page.

Got the farm down on McLeary Lane? You spoke to my wife, Helen, a few years back about listing our place."

She was so sorry to hear about Helen. She had meant to stop by. What could she do for him?

"Well, I'm thinking it's time to sell the farm," he said.

Luther and Minnie in Heaven

MINNIE LISTENED TO THE HEART MONITOR BEEPING NEXT TO HER bed. She knew it was slowing. Her children, grandchildren, and great-grandchildren had already been to her room to say good-bye. So had her rabbi, the hospice social worker, and her cousin Fanny Lozow. Her small room, in an airy wing of a well-run nursing home, was bright and stuffed with flowers and note cards. The young doctor who came in every day, uttering his usual distracted platitudes about being comfortable and then leaving after a few minutes, stayed longer this morning. For the first time, he squeezed her hand.

She was ready to move on. She'd had eighty-three good years, no complaints. She looked forward to joining her husband, Jacob, in heaven, although she hoped he wouldn't expect to be taken care of there as much as she had cared for him in this life. Minnie was done taking care of people.

But she had this other, secret wish that she had not shared with anyone. She feared her two daughters might think she was a little crazy. She wanted to see Luther, her dog.

Luther was a mutt given to her by a Catholic priest whose parish had been closing. His visit to her that day many years ago was so strange that she still went over it often in her mind.

She had never spoken to a priest before and was startled when he knocked on her door that summer day. He was tall, very thin, and was wearing his clerical collar, but also a leather jacket and a Boston Red Sox baseball cap. His red hair stuck out from under the hat and set off his bright blue eyes.

He was standing there along with a small brown and white dog on a leash. The dog was squat and ugly. The priest introduced himself as Father Matthews. "I'm here to ask you if you might consider taking my dog," he said.

The parish, which had seen dwindling attendance in recent years, was closing. Father Matthews said he was moving to an urban parish in New York City, and Luther couldn't go with him.

Minnie thought it was a joke, or a mistake, and just stared slack-jawed at the priest and this strange-looking little dog, who looked right back at her and wagged his tail hopefully.

"You're not serious, are you?" she said. "We're not really dog people."

Father Matthews smiled, as if he knew that.

"You have the kindest face," the priest said, "and I prayed that you would take Luther in. I hate to leave him. I had the sense that you two might be happy with each other. Call it a message." He looked up at the sky.

Minnie looked up also, but she saw only clouds.

Even on her deathbed, she did not understand why the

priest had come to her. It was as bewildering to her as why she eventually agreed to take Luther in.

Father Matthews had stood silently that morning, giving her time to think. Luther continued to stare at her. It was as if he knew her, was waiting for her. The kids would be shocked. She had never allowed cats or dogs or rabbits or rodents in her spotless little house. But for some reason, she now felt her heart almost literally opening up.

Father Matthews said, "All my prayers brought me here. That means something."

Minnie started to open her mouth to say no, but the word would not come out. So she said yes, and the priest handed her the leash, along with a bag of Purina Dog Chow. He leaned down, patted Luther on the head, and then walked away.

Jacob had a fit when he came home from work and found Luther dozing on the sofa, but his displeasure didn't last long. Over time, Jacob came to love Luther too, although not as much as Minnie did.

Luther ate well, grew fat and happy. He fit into the household easily, as if he had always been there. Minnie hadn't realized it, but since the kids had left, she was sometimes a bit lonely. And while she had nothing bad to say about Jacob, life with him could get a little boring. Mostly, he loved to read his paper, watch TV, and smoke his awful cigars. Luther brought a whole new focus to her life. After a few months, he was sleeping at the foot of the bed.

Luther lived with Minnie for thirteen years. Jacob had died six years after the dog arrived, and Minnie often said she would not have gotten through the loss of her husband if not for Luther. When he died, she called the New York Archdiocese, tracked down Father Matthews, and told him that Luther had passed away.

She thanked him for bringing him to her. "He's been a great comfort to me. You were right."

"Thank you for loving him," the priest said. "I will pray that you and Luther meet in Heaven." She decided not to tell the rabbi about that prayer. Jewish doctrine was a little fuzzy when it came to Heaven, and the rabbi might be wondering what she was doing chatting with a Catholic priest.

Now Minnie felt very tired. It was so quiet. The room was empty. Then the beeping slowed, and the bed filled with light and warmth, and Minnie had the most amazing sensation of feeling young and light again. She felt as if she were floating out of her tired and aching body until she couldn't hear the beeping any longer.

MINNIE RECLINED in a comfortable chair, her feet up on an ottoman. There was a small garden, the flowers rich and sweet-smelling. The air was crisp and pleasant. Songbirds were everywhere. Nothing fancy, just everything she liked.

Jacob was sitting next to her, holding her hand. They didn't live together there, but they saw each other every day, took walks together, sat and talked about their children. Somebody else took care of him.

She saw her mother and father walking together at the edge of the green lawn. Once or twice a day they waved to her and smiled. They seemed happy. She hoped she would see her children here someday too.

The days passed easily and comfortably.

One day, there was a commotion by the gate, which

swung open, and a buxom, anxious-looking woman came in calling Minnie's name. Minnie raised her hand, and the woman bounded over to her.

She was heavy-set, with curly brown hair and horn-rimmed glasses that were partially fogged up. She wore a green, blue, and red paisley cotton dress that came down to her knees. Even from a distance, Minnie could see dog hairs on it. Minnie was fastidious, and always noticed things like that. But most notably, the woman had wings. The wings were of badly frayed silk, and she wore knee-high rubber boots. She was holding an odd-looking wand, and she smelled like liver.

"I'm the angel Audrey. I've come to take you to meet Luther, as Father Matthews had prayed for."

Minnie brightened. "Father Matthews? Is he up here?"

Audrey shook her head. "Not yet. But we text."

"But Luther is here?"

"Yes, absolutely," said the angel, wiping her glasses on the edge of her dress. "But the animals have their own heaven, and it's different. The animals can't come here, but you can visit them there. If things work out, sometimes people can readopt their dogs. Or the dogs can readopt their people. It's a choice for both."

Minnie jumped to her feet—it didn't hurt at all to do that here; her knees were young again, bless them. She turned to Jacob, who was smiling, and said she would be back. She felt a flash of the old guilt, but that never lasted up here. She was free to come and go as she pleased. Jacob didn't ask to come, and Minnie didn't invite him.

"I've been assigned to the dog part of Heaven forever," Audrey said. "I've never lived on Earth myself, and I love dogs, so it's a good fit for me."

Audrey held out her hand, and Minnie took it and closed her eyes as the two of them took off into the blue sky and sailed through the air and into the clouds. Minnie looked down on a vast, beautiful terrain. There were flat plains, woods, and on all sides rolling hills pockmarked with countless caves. Streams crisscrossed the valley. There were rows of thick brush with holes dug around the roots, and clusters of old sheds, shacks, and barns.

There were no streets, houses, or big roads, just a lot of dirt paths.

"It's different," Audrey said. "That's why it has to be separate."

They landed on a large green field, and the smell was so strong that Minnie held her breath for a second. "Dog poo," she said.

"There are no cleanup laws up here," Audrey said. "The dogs can go wherever they want. It can take some adjustment for humans."

And Minnie could see that it was true, what Audrey said. All kinds of dogs, mutts of every size and description, Rottweilers, pit bulls, Afghans, Newfoundlands, Labs, shepherds, poodles, shar-peis, English bulldogs, beagles, hounds, and lapdogs wandered in and out of the caves and woods that lined the fields and bushes. There were tall and thin dogs, brown and white and black dogs, purebreds and mongrels, scary dogs and tiny loud ones. Some were dozing, others were running, growling, eating, barking, playing, or peeing or pooping wherever they pleased.

Minnie heard a familiar barking and squealing, and she turned to see Luther running up to her, wagging his tail. He shook, licked her hand, looked into her eyes. Her own eyes filled with tears as she sat down on the ground next to him.

Audrey beamed. Minnie put her arms around Luther's ugly little head and kissed him on the nose.

He was clearly pleased to see her. But she also thought that he was somewhat restrained, not as demonstrative as she remembered him. Or as she expected him to be.

"Luther, Luther, my boy, my love!" she cried out, and kept on hugging her dog. Luther wagged his tail, and then backed up a bit. He came forward and sniffed her hand, licked it, then he moved away and out toward a path that led out of the field.

"He wants to take you for a walk. He's excited to see you and wants to show you off to the other dogs. Just follow the path."

Minnie was a bit disconcerted. Something about Luther was definitely different. Audrey sensed this.

"He's been waiting for you, but he doesn't have to perform for you now. The obedience and control thing is different. You know, the way dogs down there get you to do things for them. He doesn't have to do that up here, he can do what he wants. He can just love you in the dog way."

Audrey said she would be waiting when Minnie was done visiting and ready to go back to People Heaven. Minnie turned to follow Luther toward the dirt path to take a closer look at his new home.

"One last thing," Audrey said. "Humans are not allowed off the path. There are all kinds of spikes, rocks, wire, and other obstacles that will sting and scrape you if you step off of the path. You're not allowed to go where you want. When people do go off the path, they misbehave. They get out of control. They clean up the rotten food, shovel the dog poo, and fill in the mud holes. They just mess the place up. They can't be trusted, really, to be on their own here."

Minnie followed Luther to the edge of the path, and he hopped off but walked alongside her.

Off to the right, Minnie saw countless dogs together, mating, She was startled at the sight. Most of those she knew had, like Luther, been "fixed." Minnie turned away out of decency. It was, she thought, a bit disgusting. Out of the corner of her eye, she saw Luther climbing onto the back of a hefty yellow Lab. She called out to him. "Luther! Come! Get off her!" But Luther ignored her, so she looked away and waited. After a few minutes, Luther appeared alongside the path next to her.

"You're a bad dog!" she said.

Luther cocked his head and looked at her curiously. Then he turned around and continued walking alongside the path. Minnie had never walked with him off a leash. This was strange.

Off in the distance, Minnie heard a disturbing racket, as if hundreds of dogs were fighting. She wondered what all the noise was about. Then she saw. Everywhere she looked, dogs were chasing one another, rolling and wrestling, nipping at ears, huffing themselves up, growling and barking. The din was unnerving, and she was frightened at the sight of so many dog teeth, the slashing and biting. It was awful to see.

Still, she saw no blood, just a lot of posturing and noise. Fifty yards off the path, Luther was rolling around with a Rottweiler. His teeth were bared, and he was nipping at the bigger dog. Had he lost his mind?

"Luther, get out of there! None of that!" she yelled. The two dogs squared off, shoulder to shoulder, and then Luther tore around and nipped at the other dog's tail. The larger dog gnawed on Luther's shoulder, which bled a bit. Minnie, confused and alarmed, started to run off of the path to save her dog, but she saw two strands of barbed wire and a pile of broken glass right in front of her, and she remembered Audrey's caution. She also saw that the blood had vanished, the wound healed.

"Luther, come right now!"

Luther ignored her, and disappeared into the melee.

About five minutes later, he showed up on the other side of the path. Not only was he not injured—there was some slobber on his coat—but he looked fit and happy, more relaxed than she remembered. She recalled that Luther had been something of an anxious dog, a barker. All kinds of sounds used to make him nervous—the vacuum cleaner, buses, sirens, airplanes. And he had always shied away from larger dogs.

But nothing seemed to bug him up here. In fact, Luther was out of control. He wasn't the sweet, deferential, and quiet little guy Father Matthews had brought over to the house anymore.

And Minnie realized that she'd been shouting at him ever since she saw him, and that wasn't the kind of reunion she'd been dreaming about.

"I have to say this isn't what I expected," she said, mostly to herself but in the general direction of Luther, who was walking ahead of her toward an area that seemed to be covered with garbage. The smell, like decaying meat in the summer heat, was awful.

Luther darted off again. Looking back for her every now and then, he raced to one of the piles. It looked like some kind of dead animal, and Minnie could smell it all the way from the path. Luther started rolling in the thing—it might have been a dead deer—scattering the flies and bugs and maggots.

"Get out of that right now!"

Luther moved over to a pile of garbage and started chewing on something. Minnie didn't even want to think about what it was. There were hundreds—thousands—of dogs in the vast garbage heap, rolling, eating, some even vomiting.

Minnie nearly choked at the sight. She suspected there were quite a few rabbits, chipmunks, and squirrels in the pile. She could see flies, worms, all kinds of vultures circling overhead.

So that's what they eat up here, Minnie thought. Garbage. She remembered reading somewhere that for most of their history, that's what dogs ate. Dog food wasn't even invented until the early 1960s. It didn't seem to be hurting them, at least not here.

Luther left off the garbage and hopped back up on the path. Minnie followed. Maybe now, she thought, he would just walk with her, like he used to do. Maybe he would listen to her. She saw that they were coming to another area. And the smell was different. She smelled flowers, rich soil, earth. This was better.

Minnie had been a passionate gardener down on Earth. She had never had the space for a large garden, but had done the best with what she had. And now, she was dazzled by the colorful gardens in front of her, which seemed to go on for miles. She recognized black-eyed Susans, foxglove, irises, bleeding hearts, coral bells, daffodils, pansies, petunias, marigolds, tulips, and verbena.

But as she got closer, she was horrified to see that the gardens had almost all been ravaged. Stakes were pulled out of the ground and chewed, and there were mud holes all over the place that looked as if the dogs were using them to lie in. Hundreds of bulbs had been pulled out of the ground and strewn about. There were dog droppings everywhere, and some of the flowers looked as if they'd been peed on.

Minnie had never let Luther near a garden. Back on Earth, people put up fences and warning signs. They would sometimes even call the police. She had fenced off her own garden too.

Now she didn't call Luther back or stop him, although she saw that he'd gotten into a tall stand of lilacs and was pulling them out of the ground and tossing them into the air. It almost seemed as if he were digging the garden up for her.

After a few minutes, he trotted back over to her. She leaned down to pet him, but he was pretty disgusting. His fur was matted—caked with feces, garbage, and putrid meat.

"What's gotten into you?" she asked, as he sat, wagging his tail. He was looking at her with affection, even some pleading, she thought. "What happened to my good little boy? My sweetie pie?"

Luther shook himself off, dust and detritus falling over the path, and Minnie stepped back. He walked ahead of her on the path, and they came to yet another area. This one was even stranger than the others. It looked like a series of rooms—kitchens, living rooms, dining rooms, and bedrooms—all furnished, connected to one another as far as the eye could see, stuffed with furniture. There was a sea of carpets and cushions, many of them torn, ripped, and scattered all over the floors.

Minnie gasped.

There were urine stains and dog poop on the carpet. The sofas were chewed up, pillows shredded, backs scratched and clawed. There were slobber marks on all of the windows and scratch marks on the doors. Sheets were torn into pieces and table legs strewn around. Kitchen appliances and plates and napkins were in shards everywhere.

Wow, thought Minnie, who was known for having floors you could eat off. *I would have killed Luther if he'd done this.* As she looked up, she saw that Luther *was* doing this. He was standing up on a kitchen counter, pulling open a loaf of bread and gnawing on it, scattering some of it onto the floor for some other dogs that were barking right below him.

Luther jumped off the counter and ran into a living room. He jumped up onto a sofa and tore open a cushion. Fluffy fabric flew all over the floor.

"Luther!"

But he wasn't listening to her. It seemed she couldn't command him up here, and while he was paying attention to her, and to where she was, he wasn't obeying her. He simply did as he pleased. He didn't seem to be *her* dog anymore. She wondered why she was even there.

Just then, Audrey appeared on the path in front of her. She was beaming. "Isn't this nice?"

"I wouldn't say that," Minnie said.

Audrey looked a little disturbed. "This is one of their favorite places. They just never tire of it. It's a good place to nap too." Minnie saw a poodle lying on her back, snoring amidst a bunch of mattress springs and shredded down pillows.

Audrey said she would be back shortly, and flew off again.

Minnie took a deep breath, trying to orient herself. This wasn't the cozy, idyllic reunion she had fantasized about for years. Yet there was Luther, her dog, and he sure looked happy. It occurred to her that she may not have known Luther as well as she thought. Here he was, doing things that she didn't like, and never would have allowed. But he was also doing things that *he* liked, and she had frankly never thought much about that.

Luther seemed to come and go, almost invisibly. But he returned regularly to sniff at her feet, and she would bend over and gingerly scratch his ears. He wagged his tail, seeming very pleased to be taking her for a walk.

"Luther, I love you. I've missed you terribly and waited for this day for years. I hope we can be together again."

Luther looked into her eyes, and then he was off again.

She yelled his name, but he didn't appear. She almost wanted to cry, she was so disappointed. Her heart rose in her chest. I loved that dog so much, she thought. And this love came flooding back. Their time together, their cuddles on the couch, their walks in the neighborhood. She couldn't begin to count the number of times she walked into the house, and Luther had been there to greet her. The times he had helped her get through the tough days. The loneliness he had eased. The way he got her out of the house, moving, meeting and talking with people. She suddenly felt overwhelmed with memories.

She wanted to go back, and just like that, Audrey appeared. "You ready?" she asked, and Minnie nodded. Luther was mounting a beagle in the distance. She didn't want to look.

When she got back, Jacob was sitting on the bench, smiling. Minnie was glad to sit down. She was hungry. Audrey had been right. It *had* been different. But now, Audrey told her all she had to do was call out her name whenever she wanted to see Luther again.

Minnie thanked her, gave her a hug.

"I have just one question," she said, as Audrey flapped her wings to prepare to leave. "That was Dog Heaven, right?"

"Right," said Audrey.

"Is there a Dog Hell?"

Audrey paused, then nodded. "For the dogs who hurt people and other dogs."

"What is it like?" Minnie asked.

"It's a sad place. Dogs can't run free. They're castrated or fixed. They can't have sex. They aren't allowed to squabble and they can't eat any of the things they love. In Hell, they aren't allowed to dig holes, pee where they want, or eat flowers. They can't jump on furniture or scratch at doors and windows. I've never been there, but I gather they can't even go out of doors without being tethered." She shook her head. "Creepy."

And off she went, leaving a trickle of dog hairs to fall in the fading sunlight.

A FEW DAYS LATER, Minnie went for a walk in the flower garden near the bench where she usually met Jacob. She was reminded of her visit with Luther, how different it was.

Then she called out Audrey's name, and the angel appeared instantly.

"You want to go back?" Audrey asked. "Some people don't."

Minnie nodded. "I do."

In a few minutes, they were in Dog Heaven again. Minnie started out on the path, and Luther appeared alongside of her, wagging his tail.

He did not rush up to her or squeal with delight. He did

not lick her hand or jump up or beg for treats. She did not call out to him or yell "sweetie pie" or wait for him to walk alongside her.

Luther was different from the first visit. He trotted alongside the path, and she walked steadily forward. She did not tell him to stay or come. She did not try to stop him from mounting other dogs, eating garbage, squabbling, or destroying the endless mounds of furniture. She just told herself to be quiet, and stuck to it.

This time, he stayed much closer to her. He walked with his head up, his tail straight, his chest puffed out. Once again, she could feel the love between them. But she had to concede it was different. She wasn't taking him for a walk. They were walking together.

"I love you, Luther," she said, as he ran off to eat some squalid garbage. And she waved, her eyes filling with tears. "Go be a dog."

Day in the Life of Pearl and Joan

JOAN SNIFFED THE AIR, TAKING IN THE INVITING AROMAS COMING from the grocery bags in the rear of the Subaru as the car pulled into the driveway. She savored the satisfying brew that filled the car—apples, oranges, beef, bananas, potatoes, bread, and coffee. It was so nice to have all the food you needed. She looked over at Pearl, sitting across from her in the front seat. Pearl, she saw, was doing the same thing.

Joan settled into the seat for a second, sighed, and was content. They were home. And for the first time in several hours, her joints didn't hurt.

They shopped at the same time every week: Friday, four P.M. Somehow, Pearl always knew when it was time to shop. Joan had no idea whether it was the light, or some movement or gesture of hers, but Pearl always knew when to go over to the leash hanging by the back door.

Joan was tired. She was glad shopping was over, even though it was perhaps her favorite activity, along with sitting on the sofa with Pearl. She got to meet people, see what was going on, get out of the house. She loved the ride to the market along the beautiful River Drive, past parks, dogs, a pond, bikers. She loved the smell of the breeze that drifted across Lake Michigan.

As usual, Pearl had come along and that made shopping even better. Pearl was easy company, cheerful, lovable, quiet. There wasn't much the two of them didn't enjoy doing together, and in the six years that they had been companions, there was no longer much they *didn't* do together. Joan brought Pearl along wherever and whenever she could. She had socialized her relentlessly in malls, parks, school playgrounds, along the river, in dog playgroups. Joan was pleased at how many people Pearl connected with. And Joan loved people as much or more. Pearl never met a dog she didn't like either, although some of them didn't always reciprocate.

Joan thought about the food in the car and about dinner, and a number of delicious images swirled through her head—chicken, potatoes, rice, gravy, soup. She got out of the car and waited for Pearl to follow. It was chilly. Joan shivered, but Pearl never seemed to mind the cold.

It took about fifteen minutes to haul the bags from the car—Joan and Pearl trekking back and forth together. Then everything had to be put in its proper place. There was much crinkling of paper, shifting of bags, opening and closing of cabinet doors, the soft *thwump* of the refrigerator opening and closing—Pearl sometimes stuck her head in and sniffed.

When the unpacking was done, Pearl came over to Joan for a cuddle and a kiss.

Joan loved so many things about Pearl, but if there was a single thing, it was the special love that existed between people and dogs, the powerful emotion each evoked in the other.

They knew each other so well, accepted each other so completely.

Unlike the love of some people and even of some dogs, Pearl's was absolutely unconditional. Other creatures could be fickle, cruel, unpredictable. Joan never could say for sure what was going on in Pearl's alien mind, but the love in her eyes, the acceptance, the dependability, and affection were profound. It was a tonic for Joan, which helped her forget the arthritis in her legs, and Harry's death two years earlier.

Joan had found Harry lying on the floor in the hallway. She still remembered the awful scene—the shock, the fear; paramedics storming in, trying to revive him, taking him out; the painful days that followed. She had experienced death before—the loss of her parents, others—but Harry's death was a more profound and painful wrench than she had imagined, or was in any way prepared for. Her world turned upside down. Her days were filled with fear, and an aching sense of loneliness and loss.

Joan had been with Harry for much of her life, loved him, cared for him, and it was as if the structure and rhythms of her life simply collapsed, leaving a bottomless black hole. She nearly fell apart at first. She didn't eat, sleep, or feel at peace. She didn't want to go out or see anyone.

It was better now, so much better. She was eating, walking several times a day, going out, seeing friends, even having some fun. She felt hope again, looked forward to things. Much of the healing came in the small rituals of life that she and Pearl did together—the walks, shopping, resting, driving. Joan didn't know if she would have survived without Pearl's steadfast presence. The gratitude she felt for Pearl was beyond her ability to describe, or to convey to others.

This night, as on most nights, she and Pearl had dinner

together, eating side by side. Sometimes, she left some of her food for Pearl, who always took it away, although she never saw her eat any of it.

Then, it was time for the clearing of plates and bowls. And a walk. Again, Pearl seemed to know it was time. They went out, down the front walk, and out onto the street. Some of their friends were out. Donna with Bear, Harold with Bailey. "Hey, Joan. Hey there, Pearl," Donna would always chirp. "Isn't it a wonderful evening? Bear is so happy to see you. He loves you so much, more than the other neighbors!"

Sometimes Donna was a little bit too enthusiastic for Joan, but still, she was always courteous and happy to listen to the neighborhood gossip.

Then, the ball was thrown, and this was a game Pearl almost never seemed to get bored with, although Joan's legs were getting a bit stiff with age, and the bending was difficult. Pearl dropped the ball and Joan rushed over to pick it up. It was getting chillier, and Pearl was tiring. Joan was anxious about her; Pearl could sense that. When they got home, Pearl would get her pain tablets, mixed in with some peanut butter or pudding.

Afterward, Joan and Pearl settled onto the sofa, next to each other. The wood stove was going, and the room filled with a warm glow.

Then it was time for telephone calls. First Anne, a friend, then check in with the kids, maybe talk to the grandkids.

"Mom, we're worried about you, living all alone in that house," Chip said almost every night. He felt bad about living in sunny California while she was in the chilly Midwest.

"Why don't you move out here?" he would always offer.

Joan would have hated to move. She loved her routine,

doing the same thing at the same time every day. A move would be disorienting, traumatic.

"I'm not alone," she would always respond.

"I know, I know," he said. "But she's a dog."

There was no response to that, and so they just moved on.

Joan always felt safe with Pearl. With her around, she would be watched over, taken care of, protected. If anybody came around, Pearl would notice, go investigate. Being in the house, up on a hill—the nearest neighbors separated by hardwood trees and shrubs, out of sight—could get lonely sometimes. But not with Pearl.

Whatever dangers and trials were out there in the world, they melted away here, the two of them together, in their own little corner of the world.

Chip had brought a PC on his last trip, installed it in a corner of the living room, left elaborate instructions on how to use it. But honestly, it made both of them uncomfortable. It produced new and strange noises that were disconcerting—bings, hums, clicks, and other sounds. Joan didn't like seeing it in the corner of the room. She didn't like the eerie light that flickered from the screen. It was strange and ugly and even smelled funny.

The dog got up and moved away whenever the screen lit up or beeped.

After the phone calls, it was time for a snack. Tea, scones, biscuits. The two ate delicately, nibbling at their food. This was reading time, and Joan especially enjoyed the quiet, as she did the familiarity. There was little noise, other than the shifting of human and dog against upholstery and pillows.

The computer was off. So was the TV. The phone never rang after nine P.M. There was no traffic in the street. The only sound in the house was the humming of the refrigerator and a mild buzzing from the digital table clock that was a gift last Christmas.

Joan and Pearl both nodded off, both breathing heavily, snoring slightly. Pearl snuggled against a down pillow, while Joan liked to lie against the afghan that was usually draped over the back of the sofa. The wind whispered softly against the large glass windows that Harry had put in the summer before he died.

Joan dreamed of Harry almost every night. All kinds of images of the man she had lived with streaked through her mind. Their walks, their rides in the car, their time at the ocean. Snuggling with him in bed on cold dark nights was one of the things she most missed.

At ten o'clock, Joan usually stirred, and then Pearl followed suit. The news was turned on, mostly for the weather. The rest of it was almost always bad, something dead, on fire, or angry.

Then, a final brief stroll just outside on the lawn, by the drive, a last chance for a dog to eliminate.

Finally, the walk upstairs to bed. Applying lotion to the human face, a heating pad for the sore canine joint, followed by some brushing for each. Then one lying down, pulling the covers up, turning off the light, and the other circling, pawing, plopping down in a ball, grateful for a warm, quiet spot next to a human that she loved. And then a pat, a kiss, a good night.

The night was usually uneventful, two good and quiet sleepers. Sometimes, one had to get up and use the bathroom, and sometimes, the other had to go by the back door and be let out briefly. Both of them had slightly unpredictable bladders. But most nights, they slept through until first light.

In the morning, it was Joan who stirred first, when the

first rays of sunlight crept in through the blinds. Pearl never moved until Joan did, and Joan waited for the alarm clock to come on, blaring its staticky classical music. There was no digital alarm in the upstairs bedroom, just an old-fashioned radio clock.

The day began: showering, dressing, going downstairs, opening the back door so a dog could do her business, and then breakfast. Coffee. Blood-pressure pills. Toast. Kibble mixed with a piece of chicken sausage, some joint pills, and kidney medication.

The first and longest walk of the day, around the block, down to the park, to see the other people and the other dogs, to get off leash and run a bit, as much as aging legs allowed.

Then back to the house: some cleaning, tidying, bill paying. A ride to the doctor, then to the vet for a routine checkup.

Joan handled herself well at the vet, but it nearly undid Pearl, who was nervous for hours before going.

Finally, it was time to come home, to meet Sue, an old friend who had lost her dog a couple of years earlier and who was thrilled to get on the floor and scratch the belly of another one. Sue came over for lunch every other week, alternating with her bridge club. She always brought sandwiches and treats.

Soon, it would be time for the afternoon walk. The neighbors sometimes joked that it was never really clear who was walking whom, and this was true. It never was, not to Joan and Pearl either.

And when they got home, Pearl went out to check the mail, and Joan walked slowly to her food bowl to eat the rest of the kibble she had left that morning.

The Surrender Bay

EMMA DIDN'T NEED CNN TO TELL HER SOMETHING WAS UP. EVEN before the Great Recession officially struck, she shifted her hours at the Washequa Animal Shelter before her boss could think to ask her. Washequa had once been a booming auto town, centered for decades around a GM assembly plant, but it shut down in 2008, leaving the town shell-shocked and decimated. For several months, people had been pulling up to the "Surrender Your Animals" bay of the shelter more and more often, mostly at night, because even though it wasn't their fault, they were often ashamed or heartbroken about what they had to do. The bay was created to give animal owners a safe and anonymous way to drop animals off at a shelter rather than abandon them.

One night alone, there were five dogs, six cats, a turtle, four rabbits, and a badger. The next night there were a dozen dogs and nine cats. After that, Emma decided to work nights so she could be there for the animals when they were dropped off. She didn't like to leave any animal out in the Surrender Bay all night. They were upset enough without that. She liked to get them inside, fed, registered, and settled. It was hard for her to go home and sleep if she knew animals were sitting out there. She could only imagine what their owners felt.

She remembered one beagle was sitting in his crate, howling. A note was taped onto the front of the crate door: "My name is Darryl. My owners have lost their home and their jobs. They can't really afford me anymore, and they hope you will find a great home for me and make sure that I am loved and cared for. Thank you. Please keep me alive."

Emma saw a lot of notes and messages like Darryl's, and she saved them all. One little girl wrote a letter to her surrendered Lab, Duncan, every day for two months. Emma didn't have the heart to tell her the dog had been put down.

There was a tinted glass window by the bay where Emma could look out and not be seen. Fathers came in the dead of night—Emma guessed they didn't want their kids to see their dogs and cats leave—and hurriedly, almost furtively, put the animals into one of the dozen large crates that were left open by the staff. There was a donation box next to the crates, but most of the time people were so eager to get away, they didn't put anything in it. Some probably couldn't afford to. She saw a woman fall to her knees sobbing as she hugged her cat for the last time. There was an elderly couple surrendering their ancient dachshund, telling him softly they were moving to a facility that couldn't take him, thanking him for his love and loyalty. A young girl in tears left her parrot in a cage, then rushed back to the car where her mom yelled for her to hurry up.

Every so often, the tortured families returned in the

morning in a panic to get their animals back. "We just couldn't do it," said one mother, who came with her two children to get their mutt back when the shelter opened at six A.M. Emma was still there, about to tag the dog and put him in quarantine. The shelter rules said that once a dog was surrendered, people had to go through the whole adoption process—including a $60 fee and interview—before they could get the animal back, but Emma looked the other way once in a while.

"I don't have a job, and I'm not sure where we're going to be living," said the woman. "But I guess it will have to be a place that takes dogs." Her kids, both girls, were crying, hugging their dog for dear life. Emma stood in the bay and waved good-bye as their battered Taurus pulled away.

Two weeks after Emma started working nights, it was all over the news—the stock market was crashing, unemployment was soaring. There would be more animals coming into the Surrender Bay.

The shelter's budget had been slashed and slashed, the staff reduced by a fourth, and even though Emma worked sixty hours a week, she was on the payroll as a part-timer—$13 an hour and no benefits. But she felt the animals needed her more than ever, and this was true. And she had something few people had—she loved her work, every minute of every day. In this job, Emma saw, you felt needed, for sure. It was pure. The animals needed you and were grateful for every scrap of food or cuddle that they got.

She didn't keep dogs and cats of her own because she knew then there wouldn't be room for emergencies, or for the animals she liked to give an occasional treat by getting them out of the shelter for a night. She did this especially with dogs and cats she knew were likely to be put down. Her own Last Suppers.

The shelter was a flat single-story building that had been donated to the town by a machine shop that had once occupied the space. It had a reception area, a surgery, a meeting place where people could spend time with the animals, a "containment" room for dangerous or sick dogs or cats, and various rooms that held between fifteen and thirty crates of various sizes. There was also a row of exercise pens in the rear of the facility. The place was swabbed and scrubbed twice daily, but it still had that shelter smell—a combination of blood, fur, vomit, and fecal waste mixed with disinfectant and alcohol—that had woven itself into the walls.

The shelter held 140 animals, and had been filled up for months. Now it was overflowing. Crates were stacked in the hallways and reception areas. So many animals were being abandoned that they couldn't close the shelter, yet they didn't really have the money to fund it either. So the staff simply did whatever it took. Some days, Emma and the other employees drove around in the shelter van to local pet stores—they often went to the wealthier Cleveland suburbs an hour to the north—to beg and borrow kibble and canned food. One pet-supply chain let them have damaged bags of food, or food that had been returned for one reason or another.

The staff had come to call the end of the week "Black Friday" because that was when sick, "dangerous," or unadoptable animals were euthanized. Emma forced herself to look at the list of animals posted in the surgery every Friday morning. Sometimes there were twenty or thirty names on the list. The shelter did everything they could to find homes for the animals, but it was tough. And getting tougher. Many more animals were coming in than going out. Room had to be made for the new ones who were being surrendered every day.

Emma made it an article of faith to say good-bye to all of the animals, taking them out of their cages for a final pet if she could, and if there was time. She was determined that no animal leave the world without some human affection or a proper farewell. Some Fridays, she assisted the vets, holding the cats and dogs, closing their eyes while the needles went in, taking the bodies out and treating them with dignity. A cremation service collected them. Emma put a name tag on every animal before they were collected.

People were often shocked to learn the reality of life at the shelter. As Sandy, the director, told them, "We're not a no-kill shelter. We can't afford to be." There was hardly any such thing as a "no-kill shelter." There were shelters that did their own killing, and shelters that sent animals away to be killed, or didn't accept any whom they might have to kill. These days, almost no publicly funded shelter could afford to care for animals for years at taxpayer expense.

Emma remembered one father she encountered when she still worked days and interacted with the customers. The man grabbed her by the shoulders and put his face close to hers. "Can you imagine what it feels like to be in this position?" he had said quietly, but with a kind of smoldering rage. "To be so low that you have to bring the family dog in here because you can't afford vet bills and dog food? To face my kids when I go home and tell them I sent their dog away?"

Emma forced herself to look this man in the eye. "Look, Mr.," she said, her voice shaking, "I'm sorry for you and for your dog. But this is not my fault. We're both doing the best we can."

The man looked at her for a second, then turned, got into his pickup, and drove away, leaving his confused German shepherd with Emma.

When Emma got discouraged, she thought of the many happy scenes. The children who left holding dogs and cats in their arms, the lucky animals who found a family. Saying good-bye to them was a different kind of farewell, and they carried her through the other times.

One early evening shortly after Emma's shift began, she and her coworker Sam heard a roar coming off the highway that separated the mostly abandoned strip mall from the animal shelter. Emma looked out the rear window and saw a dozen big black motorcycles thundering down the road. At first, it didn't occur to her that they would be coming to the shelter, but the bikes slowed down and rumbled toward the entrance, belching smoke as they approached.

Emma heard the barking start up—the animals hated the noise. Soon, there was a din of barking, howling, and yelping that seemed to rattle the shelter.

"Jeez," said Sam. "The ground is shaking." Emma saw that the lead driver had an animal crate fastened to the rear of his bike.

Emma, never one for confrontation, scurried back to one of the crate rooms, where she could busy herself feeding or socializing or medicating one of the dogs and the cats. Maybe tonight she would visit Brownie, the fat old golden whose elderly owners had had their home foreclosed. She needed to have her bandages changed—she'd had a cancerous growth removed—and Emma doubted the shelter would be able to keep her alive much longer.

She heard some noise in the reception area.

Sandy, the director, was on duty. She could talk to the

bikers. Emma could see the black leather jackets, long hair sticking out from under the helmets, jeans and studded boots. No way was she going to talk to them.

She saw Sam go to the reception area to help Sandy out.

Emma let Brownie out of her crate and kissed the old dog on the nose, and then gently lifted her up on the examining table. She carefully took her dressing off—she couldn't be interrupted now—and took some liver treats out of her pocket. Emma bought them with her own money at the local PetSmart. The shelter couldn't afford to buy treats.

Emma didn't have the heart to ask Sandy, but she guessed, from her experience, that this Friday would be the day Brownie would be put down. Nobody in Washequa was going to adopt a dog with cancer, not a twelve-year-old. And the shelter couldn't justify paying for more surgery for her. There were younger, healthier dogs to save, some who might find homes.

While Emma put a fresh bandage on and gave Brownie her antibiotics, Sam came in, looking flushed and angry.

"What happened?"

"That biker, a macho jerk, came with a large, brownish cat, and he said he wanted to leave the cat but he wanted to know for sure that she would find a home. When Sandy said she couldn't promise that, he nearly put his fist through the wall and called her a bitch. He said she had to find a home for the cat or he would chew the place up.

"I told him to chill out, and two of his thugs came toward me until Macho Man stopped them, just held up his hand. Sandy threatened to call the police and told me to go get a carrier for the cat. I didn't want to leave, but I saw she wanted me to get out of there." Sam went into one of the storerooms to get a travel carrier.

Emma felt a surge of anger. But she remembered Sandy saying they had to think of the animals, not the people.

Sam, still visibly upset, hurried back into the reception area with a big plastic carrier.

A short while later, Emma heard the cycles roar off.

She ventured out into the hallway, but there was nobody there. She walked down the hall to the Surrender Bay area, where new animals to the shelter were kept in quarantine for two weeks. It was feeding time, and that was part of Emma's job. She looked at her watch and saw it was time to give the new arrivals their antibiotics too. She went into the medicine cabinet for fresh syringes and the medicine vials.

She also reached for one of the food bags before heading down the hallway. She heard a male voice from inside the new-arrival room, but it wasn't Sam's. She froze. The hallway lights were kept off as a budget-saving measure, turned on only when necessary. She knew she couldn't be seen as she tiptoed to the window and peered in. She barely allowed herself to breathe. Slowly, she put the food and medical equipment down on the floor and edged closer.

An enormous man in a black leather motorcyle jacket—his long black hair down to his shoulders—was sitting on the floor in a corner in profile to her.

An empty cat carrier sat at his feet.

He looked to be in his early thirties. He had a thick neck and broad shoulders and a big belly that pushed against his weathered black jacket. The jacket was covered with studs, and he had a ring hanging from one side of his nose. She saw a tattoo—a dragon's head—protruding from his chest onto his neck.

A large tortoiseshell cat with the greenest eyes she'd ever seen was sitting in his lap. The door to the crate next to the two of them was open. The glass was thick, but his voice was loud and guttural. She could hear him.

"Hey," he growled, "I'm sorry to be leaving you here. I'll come back for you if I can. They say they'll try to find a good home for you. But I don't know if they're bullshitting me or not. I don't know what's gonna happen."

The cat snuggled in his lap and looked up into his eyes.

Emma didn't move. The man seemed to look the cat over carefully, as if wanting to remember every detail.

Emma wanted to get away, but her legs didn't quite know how to move.

The biker looked back at the cat and stroked her chin.

"You're a great cat. I can't believe some of the rats and mice you got. I'll miss you."

Emma could see that he was choked up.

"I'm sorry," he said.

The cat looked up at him again curiously. His words were abrupt, but his tone wasn't. Emma had been through a lot of these surrenders, and people rarely wanted to be alone with the animals they were leaving. Giving them up was hard enough.

"I have to leave, Cleo," he said. The cat was curled up comfortably in his arms. It was always tough, Emma thought, when people realized how much the animals trusted them, how safe they felt with them. That made it harder to let them go.

"We have to move. No more jobs here, and we don't know where we're going. The landlord put us out. Can't put you through that kind of a trip."

He looked up at the ceiling, and Emma was surprised to see tears streaming down both sides of his face. He's about had it, Emma thought. She had seen it before. There was a point where people just had to get out. He was about there.

Emma shook her head, fidgeting with the bottom of her green smock.

He put the cat back in the crate and got up quickly, starting toward the door. Emma left the food and supplies on the floor and backed up quickly, stepping into one of the other new-arrival rooms. She heard the biker open the door and head out into the hallway. Seconds later, she heard Sam's voice saying, "Hey, you aren't supposed to be in here," and then she heard a bellow and some cursing and a loud noise.

She ran out into the hallway and flipped the lights on. She saw the biker with one arm on Sam's shoulder, and Sam, looking white as a ghost, pinned to the glass wall.

"Who the hell are you to tell me I can't go say good-bye to my cat? It's my cat, and you people can't even promise me you'll find a home for her, and now you tell me to get out!"

The biker was red with rage, and Sam, as skinny as a popsicle stick, was nearly paralyzed. Dogs were barking all over the shelter.

Without thinking, Emma strode up to the biker.

"Hey!" she said, and both men turned toward her. She put her hand on the biker's wrist and pulled his arm off Sam's shoulder.

"I saw how much you love your cat. I know how hard it is to let her go. How angry you must be, and frustrated. We see it all the time. But you just can't take it out on us. We'll care for her. We'll love her. We're her only chance."

Sam looked at her as if she'd fallen out of a spaceship.

She moved forward a step.

The biker was breathing normally now, and he stepped back.

"Sorry," he said to Sam. "I just lost it there."

Sam nodded, then offered his hand. The two shook.

Emma put her hand on the biker's shoulder.

"Mister, I know you feel guilty. But you shouldn't feel that way—what's your name?"

"Howie," he said.

"You're one of the good ones," she said. "Some people just abandon their cats on the street. We have a whole room of those. You thought to bring her here. It's the best you can do. We'll take good care of her. You should feel good about what you've done."

Howie met her gaze. "She was like our kid, you know? We move from place to place; we aren't very connected, but she's special to us."

Emma nodded. "Listen to me, Howie. Give yourself permission to let her go. The people who come here are good people in bad situations. We have to remember that."

"What's your name?" he asked.

"Emma."

His eyes filled with tears again.

"What are the chances—"

Emma shook her head. "We never know. But she's a beautiful, healthy cat, and that's good news. She's got a chance. A lot of them don't."

"And how long—"

"Look, Howie. You have to walk away and not look back. You gave her the best life you could for as long as you could. You start over every single day. Every day there's a win, every day there's a loss. You have to go on. We'll take it from here. You're not leaving her alone or starving on the street."

Howie listened, looked at Emma more closely, and nodded. Then he went into the new-arrival room one last time. He opened the crate, held Cleo's face up to his, hugged her, put her gingerly back in the crate—she fought him a bit, but he managed to get her in—and then he shut the door and stood up.

Tears still streaming down his cheeks, he walked quickly back out into the hallway, past Sam, and over to Emma.

Leaning forward, he kissed her on the cheek.

"Thank you, Emma," he said, and left.

It was evening, and the shelter was at its quietest. The animals had been fed and medicated. There were still a few hours before the cars would start pulling up to the Surrender Bay, and it would begin filling up with newly homeless pets.

Emma had looked at the Black Friday list again, and afterward, she shook her head, took a deep breath, and choked back a few tears.

She told Sam she was going out for a few minutes. He'd asked her if she wanted to join him for dinner on the way home, something the two of them did once or twice a week, as both lived alone and often—mostly—ended up talking about the animals at the shelter anyway. Emma didn't even know where Sam lived.

But tonight, Emma said no. She had other plans. Sam smiled. He understood.

She drove to the Burger King a few miles down the road. The assistant manager knew her there and waved. "You want the usual?"

She nodded, and he ordered her a Giant Whopper, the

big kind with three slices of beef, gobs of cheese and mayonnaise, lettuce, tomato, and bread. She also got a small tomato-wedgie salad and a Diet Pepsi.

Emma drove the short distance back to the shelter, now locked up and deserted, except for the din the animals made whenever she opened the doors, and made her way to the holding room where Brownie's crate was. The room was dark, and she heard the whimpering of the animals—six mutts, two beagles, an aging German shepherd, four cats, some Lab-mix puppies, and two pit bulls unlikely to find a home.

After the initial barking and yowling and mewing—"It's just me," she said, "ssssssh,"—she turned on the lights, still clutching the greasy bag of food.

She walked to the far corner, took out a blanket, and spread it on the floor, then opened the last crate on the left.

"Hey, Brownie," she called out quietly, "you free for dinner?"

Away to Me

ZIP WAS EXCITED. THE FARMER HAD JUST COME OUT OF THE FARM-house. First thing every morning, before the mist was burnt off by the summer sun, he emerged from the house and called out, "Hey, Zip, let's get working." He quickly ducked into the barn and returned again with feed for the goats and chickens. Then it was time to move the sheep from the barn to the outer pasture, where they would graze until the sun got too strong.

Zip ran back and forth in front of the sheep, which were all struggling to their feet, baaing loudly. Zip loved work more than anything except, perhaps, sunning herself or getting her head and ears scratched. The sheep were her responsibility, she watched over them day and night. It gave her life focus and connected her to the ancient ritual of working with a human being, and serving him.

Some of these characteristics were in her bones, but she had learned much more from Fly, the farmer's border collie, who had grown up with Zip on the farm, and who had herded the sheep with great energy and skill until she lay down with them in the pasture one summer night and died in her sleep.

Zip, who was not a border collie, was lonely. She missed her companion, but she had watched Fly and studied her, so she knew what to do. Fly and Zip had been inseparable, working the sheep day and night, protecting them together. Fly had been generous, working happily with Zip, passing on her experience, showing her how to understand and move sheep, and Zip had taken to the work as naturally as Fly had. Zip was not quite as agile or quick as Fly, but she was determined and had great poise and authority, and the sheep did what she wanted them to do.

Zip loved the way the sheep reacted, their heads going up when she and Fly had appeared in the mornings, how they'd bunched together anxiously, how they'd come to associate Fly and Zip with grass and moved eagerly along with them.

One or two would always break away for something greener, and Fly, so quick, would head them off, turn them, nip them on the nose if necessary. Zip saw how easily the sheep could panic—when a coyote appeared, or another animal moved in the brush, or lightning struck a tree in the forest, or a plane roared overhead—and she and Fly would sense this, get ahead of them, turn them, keep them together, calm them.

Zip saw how the sheep's heads would go down when they found good grass, and then go up when they were full and it was time to return to the shade, to water and the safety of the barns and fences. The lambs loved to play, refusing to be herded, and they made their mothers crazy with worry and responsibility. It was hard to keep them together with the flock and away from dangers and predators.

Zip learned to be careful around the rams, who could get belligerent and territorial, and would often butt her if she wasn't paying attention.

In the middle of the night, especially on hot nights when the farmer let her stay in the pasture outside the barn, Zip would stand in front of the herd, watching for the coyotes that often came creeping around. At the sight of them, she would get to her feet and move forward to confront them, making as much noise as she could, staying between them and the herd. She sensed they were cowards and opportunists, and when she came forward to confront them, they fled.

The farm sat in a flat lush valley surrounded by soft green hills. There was a big white farmhouse, and a pasture for milk cows, and a milking barn. Zip was not allowed near the cows. They were dangerous, as they would kick her. The sheep were in a larger pasture to the south, with their own gates, fences, and barns. They lived outside almost all of the time, except when it was raining heavily or very cold. Twice a year, the farmer lambed. Two or three times a year, trucks came and took some of the sheep away—Zip never knew where, and the farmer always locked her up in one of the barns when this happened. When she came out, she would look for them, but they would be gone. They never came back.

The sheep were different from dogs, or even from cows. They were simple. They ate, chewed their cuds, slept. They never anticipated what might happen to them, or remembered what had already happened. They never quite understood that Zip was there to take care of them, so she often had to reestablish her authority. They had little memory and often made the same mistake twice. Falling into holes, getting snagged on fences, tripping on rocks, running into fence posts. They needed watching.

The farmer was a tall, weathered-looking man. He wore the same thing just about every day—lace-up waterproof boots, Carhartt overalls, a plaid flannel shirt, a hooded sweatshirt with a woolen cap. He was a gentle, confident man. He never panicked, or got upset, which Zip appreciated. Over time, the two of them had built a strong and comfortable relationship. The farmer always spoke to her clearly and softly. He'd grown up on the farm, as had his father and grandfather, and he knew every inch of it. And he understood animals—livestock as well as dogs. He knew how to talk to them, knew what made them nervous and what calmed them. His farm was a well-run place, and a sense of that permeated the barns and pastures and was absorbed in the animals who, like the farmer, generally went about their business and did what they were expected to do.

Zip loved working with the farmer, loved his smell, his gentleness, and most of all, the work that he brought her. When he commanded, "Away to me!" or "Get the sheep!" her heart felt like it would come right out of her chest, and she took off as quickly as she could run, trying to get around the herd so that they would stay together, and she could follow them up to the pasture and stand guard.

Sometimes, Zip could sense, the farmer got frustrated. Zip was not as fast as Fly had been, not as instinctive. Sometimes the sheep got ahead of her, or didn't turn, or ran off to the far rise of the pasture. The farmer would shake his head, mutter a bit, and go up and get them with Zip. He never yelled at her, though she could sense his disappointment.

But Zip knew she was, without a doubt, the smartest

thing on the farm with four legs. She knew the sheep far better than any farmer could. She could smell things the farmer couldn't even imagine existed. She saw their eyes when they were frightened, saw their heads go up when they were hungry, heard the sound of pain when their hooves were cracked, could read the messages when they called out to one another, or to their lambs. She knew the smell of the ewes when they were pregnant, understood when they were about to give birth.

She also heard the farmer's footsteps hit the floor in the morning, the running water in the shower. She could read his mind before he even conceived his own thoughts.

ZIP'S LIFE had not always been this good. It had taken her a while to trust this farmer. She had been born on a nearby farm, with a different kind of farmer, who was angry and frightening. He threw rocks and used a stick; and Zip was, to this day, fearful of sticks even to the point of biting anyone who came near her with one.

Fly had come to that farm as a puppy, and grown up right alongside Zip. Zip and Fly had quickly grown attached to each other. Life was rough there and each provided the only companionship for the other. Food was not always regularly available, and the farmer was brusque, angry, and could sometimes turn impatiently violent.

But then Zip's life changed. The farm was sold. A truck came, and a rope was tied to her neck, and she was dragged and pushed into the truck and taken to another farm. She didn't know then that Fly was going too.

The new farmer was so different. He was gentle and spoke to her by her name. He fed her twice a day, brushed her, talked to her, scratched her ears and, once in a while, even kissed her on the nose. He brought her treats, all kinds of cookies and feed. It was a different kind of life, but it still centered around work. Every morning, Zip and Fly marched the sheep out to pasture, and stayed with them all day, and every evening they brought them back, sleeping near them all night.

From the first, Zip wanted to sleep in the house, to follow the farmer there. She knew there were good things to eat there; she could smell them. And she wanted to come in especially when it was cold or raining, but the farmer always turned and held up his hand as he latched the pasture gate. "Only people in the house," he said.

And by now, years later, Zip knew all of the farmer's commands by heart: "Come bye"; "Away to me"; "That'll do, Zip"; or "Let's bring 'em in." She knew when it was time to take the sheep out, and she knew when it was time to bring them in, to move them into a different pasture, or keep them in the barn.

At night, when the sheep were well-fed and sleepy, the farmer would give her a biscuit, scratch her head and back, and thank her for her hard work that day.

But one day, a border collie a lot like Fly appeared on the farm. At first, Zip was excited. But this was a different dog, and unlike Fly, the dog seemed to pay no attention to Zip. He was focused entirely—almost obsessively—on the sheep and on the farmer.

He was a black and white dog, sleek and fast and low to the ground. Not at all like Zip, who was large and had heavier bones and big ears. The new dog watched the farmer closely, and reacted so swiftly to the farmer's commands. The sheep reacted powerfully to the new dog, bunching together, staring at him, locking eyes in the same way that Zip had seen Fly do but that she had never quite been able to figure out herself.

The farmer paid a lot of attention to the new dog, taking him out into the farmyard, working with him, getting him to lie down, sit, and stay, things he had never really taught Zip to do.

Zip was confused. She still took the sheep out in the mornings and brought them back. But after that, the farmer left her behind. He put her in the barn and worked only with the new dog.

Zip was more and more disturbed. She became anxious, sometimes refusing to leave the sheep and not allowing herself to be brushed. She wouldn't take treats or permit the farmer to come close anymore.

One day, he came and talked to her.

"Hey, girl," he said, "I know this is upsetting to you, and I see that you're unhappy. But I need this dog here. He's a sheepdog, a working dog. He can do things you can't do, although you're a good girl. I'm expanding the flock, opening a new pasture. There'll be more lambs. It's just too much for you. There will always be a place for you. You'll get used to it. It's for the good of the farm."

Zip didn't understand anything the farmer had said, although she did pick up the reassurance and affection in his tone. He was telling her things were okay, trying to calm her. But she knew she was being replaced. She had lost her job.

Suddenly, the rhythms and routines of her life were all jumbled. She couldn't relax, and could barely sleep. Things were just not right. The new dog was always with the farmer, seeing the things Zip had only heard and never quite understood.

Then one day, the new dog—who was called Red—followed the farmer out past the farmhouse and into the pasture, trailing slowly behind him.

Zip raced back and forth in alarm, but the farmer didn't react to her, he just continued speaking to Red. All kinds of images flashed through Zip's mind—sheep running and panicking, coyotes skulking around. She felt more protective of the sheep, and of her own work caring for them, than she ever had.

When the farmer opened the gate, Red rushed right by Zip, as if she were invisible, and headed toward the sheep. At first, Zip was paralyzed and confused. Then her instincts kicked in. Zip would protect the sheep.

She charged in front of Red, lowered her head, and bit him in the shoulder. He yelped, and she bored into him, making as much noise as she could. Red seemed shocked. He was stunned, in pain, and he ran back out the pasture gate, toward the farmer.

Zip was proud of herself, and so relieved that he was gone. She expected praise, as she had always received when she protected the sheep. But the farmer was angry. He threw a stick at her—something he had never done—and yelled at her in an angry voice. "No, Zip! What's wrong with you? Bad! Bad!"

Things went from bad to worse for Zip. The farmer and Red returned to the pasture the next day, and Zip again charged toward the gate. The farmer yelled again, and he put a rope on Zip and pulled her into the barn. He was angry, shouting. "What's come over you, girl? You can't be out here if you're going to be this way."

He locked her in one of the rooms in the barn.

Zip was crushed. She understood that she had failed, but

she had no sense of how. She had done what she'd always done. But still she was being shunted aside for this other dog.

She stayed in the barn for days, anxious and angry, as she heard the dog and the farmer come and go. She cried out again and again, but to no avail.

The farmer brought her food there, but he would not let her out. And she refused to eat, or to be consoled. She rushed toward the door, tried to nose it open, barrel through it, but she couldn't get out.

Zip missed her work terribly, and was deeply worried about the sheep. She became lethargic, refusing her food, even treats, backing off whenever the farmer came near her. How could she be shut up in a barn while the sheep were outside in the pasture, in danger?

She knew the farmer and Red were going out to the sheep two or three times a day, but she could not understand the shouts and commands and movements she could feel and hear. The sheep were not panicking, running, or being attacked. They were moving out to pasture, and they were coming back. Some of them called out to her, and she responded.

But Zip heard no cries of pain or alarm, smelled no blood.

The farmer kept coming in to see her. He was worried. She sensed that. She closed her eyes and dreamed of Fly, of their herding days together. This dog was different. She knew from the way the farmer acted, from the way Red acted, that she and Red would not be working together.

After several days, a familiar pickup pulled into the farm. It belonged to a man the farmer called "Doc Osterhaudt," the man who stuck needles in her and looked into her eyes. She always tried to hide when she heard his truck.

Usually, the farmer locked her up before the truck came so she couldn't run off.

Then the two came into the barn, and the man called Doc looked her over, felt her nose, and checked her eyes. He smiled, but the farmer seemed anxious. He told Doc about the attack on Red, the nervousness, the refusal to eat, the balkiness. How Zip had even nipped at his hand.

"She's fine," Doc said. He leaned over to pat Zip on the head, but she pulled back. She was having none of it. He reached into his pocket and offered her a cookie, but she snorted and refused.

"Your problem is that she doesn't know she's a donkey. She thinks she's a dog. You've been working the sheep and she's come along, so she thinks she's herding them. She doesn't know better. And now you've brought another dog in to work the sheep, which she thought was *her* job. It's like she was just fired."

The farmer laughed. Of course. Zip had always come along when he took the sheep out to pasture, and again when he brought them back.

"What can I do?"

Doc packed up his bag and headed for his truck. "Get another donkey. Then she'll figure out who she is. And she'll let the dog do his work."

SOME DAYS LATER, another truck pulled into the farm. A young male donkey, a small, four-legged creature with large ears and a high-pitched bray, got off the truck and was led into the pasture.

Zip rushed over and snorted at it, nipped it on the shoulder, kicked her rear legs at it. She was uncertain whether to be enraged or terrified. She was both.

Then Zip and this new creature—his name was Jimmy—were put into the barn together, and the two of them didn't come out for days. The farmer dropped hay in through one of the barn windows, leaving the two to get acquainted.

When Zip and the new donkey emerged after nearly a week, she was calm again. She and Jimmy trotted out to pasture with the sheep, but though they grazed with them, she and the other donkey spent the day mostly together. Often, they went off to find some weeds and scrub by themselves, and they chewed quietly and peacefully together for hours. At night, the two of them went back into the barn and lay down on the pile of straw together, sleeping until the rooster woke them in the early morning. Sometimes at night, the farmer would bring his radio into the barn, and he would sing to Zip and Jimmy as he fixed some of the equipment, pausing occasionally to give them oats and apples.

Zip still missed Fly, and thought of her often.

But it was a good life again.

Guardian Angel

HARRY ARCHIBALD AND HIS WIFE, SALLY, MOVED TO NAPLES, Florida, from Columbus, Ohio, a few months after Harry attended the forty-fifth reunion of his Vietnam War infantry division. Seeing his old buddies, Harry was reminded that life was too short to keep freezing every winter. It was time for some fun. He and Sally had earned it.

In short order, they got a used two-bedroom trailer in a meticulously maintained retirement community around a small man-made lake; a custom-made wooden motorboat to putter around the lake with; a Dodge minivan with powerful air-conditioning; a Walmart patio set with a table, four chairs, and umbrella; a large-screen HDTV; and a pug named Gus.

The Archibalds were what some called "good people." They were cheerful, positive, and generous. Sally volunteered at local nursing homes, reading to the patients, bringing cookies and soda, and Harry was the kind of guy who mowed the lawns of widows and offered total strangers rides to the market. They were good neighbors, the kind of people you left your keys with and asked to feed your cats.

Harry and Sally had had a dog once before. They'd gotten a pound dog from a local shelter years earlier when the kids were young, but he died after a few years and they never got around to getting another one. They were so busy working and raising their family, they didn't think they could devote enough time to another animal. But now was their chance.

They called Gus their surrogate child, since none of their children were nearby. The neighbors adored him too. You couldn't walk Gus or take him to the post office without touching off a small riot. It was, Sally joked, like having a kid again, without having to actually have the kid.

The couple was crazy about their little motorboat. Every afternoon, Sally would make sandwiches, and they would set off in the tiny lake. They would putter around and pull into the community marina, buy some soda, iced tea, and ice cream, and have lunch with some of their neighbors. Harry especially loved piloting the little boat, turning up the tiny outboard as far as it would go. "Like Lord Nelson," he would say to Sally, and both of them would smile.

Gus would always come along. He loved to sit in the front and bark at the other boats, as if ordering them out of the way. He went everywhere with Harry—on walks, drives into town, even to the card games at the VFW.

One afternoon, as Harry and Sally were taking their evening walk around the edge of the lake, Harry turned to Sally and said, "I think Gus is our guardian angel. I think he came here to watch over us."

Sally teared up. "Harry, I've never heard you talk that way about anything, not even me."

Sally loved to look out the trailer window on sunny afternoons and see Harry lying on a deck chair, listening to the radio or reading his paper, while Gus perched on the edge of the chair and looked out imperiously over the trailer park, daring anyone to bother them or come near. Harry usually read Gus the headlines, especially the outrageous ones—scandals, political news, sports-contract negotiations. Sally was pretty sure that Harry read Gus every word written about Tiger Woods and his troubled married life.

Harry had always expected to go first, planned for that, so he was surprised when Sally started to feel poorly and felt a sharp pain in her abdomen. He had a bad feeling about it.

The pancreatic cancer was diagnosed right away, and their idyllic life abruptly changed. Death on the battlefield was one thing. Death in your family was quite another. Harry was, he knew, going to be tested in a completely new way.

He wasn't really prepared for the nightmares of the health-care system. The doctors put Sally on an aggressive regimen of chemotherapy. Next, the doctor recommended surgery, and Sally had one operation, then another. She lost her hair. She couldn't swallow. She couldn't sleep. She was nauseous much of the time. One of Harry's neighbors urged him to consider a hospice, but Harry felt guilty even thinking about it, like he was giving up on Sally.

The medications piled up, as did the medical equipment in their home—the pill bottles, feeding tubes, special pillows, a hospital bed, specially made chairs, a wheelchair, and a walker. Meanwhile, Sally got only weaker and more uncomfortable.

Gus seemed to get what was happening. He went to the doctor with Harry and Sally, waiting in the car, looking out the window. When she felt bad, he sat on Sally's bed, near her feet. He seemed to know when to get close and when to stay away.

And he hovered near Harry like a spirit. Harry never wanted Sally to see him discouraged, so he took Gus for walks when he needed to step away. He did his best thinking out on the boat, and the dog always came along too. He talked to Gus, mentioned the hospice to him, wondered about how much to put Sally through. He had the odd sense that Gus was listening, and got the gist of it, even if he didn't understand the words.

Sally slept in a hospital bed in the living room. Harry had moved their regular bed so he could be near her, and Gus moved back and forth all night between the two beds. "You're my angel," Sally said to the dog one night, just before falling asleep.

The kids came and went, and were loving and helpful, but they had lives elsewhere, and Harry and Sally had been rigorous about not intruding on them. But it was Gus who was there for Harry every minute.

After a year of surgery and chemo, the doctors recommended Sally be put in a nursing home. That afternoon, Harry took Gus out into the boat. "We're at the end, boy. I can't put her through more of this." Sally begged Harry to let her die at home, not in a home or hospital, and so Harry called the hospice. A social worker came and talked to them while Gus sat and listened as if he were part of the team. It was decided that Sally would stay at home.

Harry and Sally both came to terms with her impending death, and she died holding his hand, just as she had wished. She always said Harry was the last thing she wanted to see on this earth. Gus watched from the foot of the bed, and just before she died, he jumped off and went into the other bedroom and curled up on the floor, where he stayed for hours. When he finally came out, he attached himself to Harry like Krazy glue.

After Sally died, Gus began sleeping next to Harry in bed, curling up on his feet, sitting in his lap while Harry stared at his flat-screen TV through the long nights. When Harry was drained, he would get into the boat with Gus, and head out into the lake, or take a walk on one of the community paths, or just ride out to the beach to listen to the waves and look at the morning sun.

Even with Medicare and Harry's veteran's benefits, he was left with $30,000 in medical bills and paying them off had just about wiped him out. If necessary, he'd get a job at Walmart, or pump gas. Even at his age, he could still work, and he would if he had to. War was one kind of sacrifice for his country. This was another.

Harry was not a complainer. He was always careful to be cheerful when his kids called.

"I'm fine," he would say. "Moving on with my life. I miss your mom very much, but she wouldn't want me to mope."

Still, the calls from his kids made him sad. He knew there was something missing. Everybody was always fine, everybody always recited what they did that day, what the kids did that day, but Harry wished there had been more connection, that his daughters and son would open up to him more. But, hell, he had never done it, so why should they?

Harry loved the boat rides with Gus in the afternoon and was determined to keep taking them. At the marina, he would sit with Gus and toss him bits of the sandwich he'd brought along. Harry didn't often have an appetite.

Once, at church, he thanked God for Gus. "I don't know

what would have happened to me without that little dog. Thank you, Lord."

By now, the joke had become an article of faith. Gus was, without doubt, an angel, Harry believed, sent by God to help Sally and him get through the end of their lives with dignity and peace. When all was said and done, there was nobody else. There was just Gus, every day, every night.

When Gus began losing weight and vomiting, Harry assumed it was something the dog had eaten. The vet kept him overnight, the first time Harry had been alone in Florida. It was a tough night.

The vet called him the next morning with bad news. Gus had kidney disease, a narrowing of the renal blood vessels. It was potentially fatal. Without treatment, Gus would lose weight, appetite, and his kidneys would likely fail.

Harry's heart sank. He could not yet comprehend life without Sally. And to lose his guardian angel as well?

The vet said there was one choice, but it was a long shot. There was a veterinary kidney specialist in Fort Lauderdale who could put stents in Gus's arteries, perhaps save his life. The problem was that the procedure was complex, and expensive, and sometimes it took two or three operations. And it didn't always work. He gave Harry the number of the practice in Fort Lauderdale and hung up.

This time, there was no insurance, and nothing left in the bank.

He picked Gus up in his arms and took him out to the boat. He lay the dog's listless little body on a boat cushion and flicked the ignition. The boat roared to life and quickly chugged out into the middle of the lake. There, Harry turned the engine off, and looked down at Gus, who stared at him with his big black eyes. Harry felt tears in his own eyes.

"Are you hurting, Gus? I won't let you suffer unnecessarily." *I'll be your angel,* he thought.

The lake was still, his voice echoed across it. Fish bubbled up to the surface, and herons watched for fish, and ducks bobbed their heads under the water looking for food. Harry had never felt so alone in his life, not even in Vietnam.

He motored back to the dock behind the trailer and picked Gus up to carry him back to the house. Gus had already lost a lot of energy. Once inside, Harry put some kibble down, but the dog wasn't hungry.

Harry called the number in Fort Lauderdale. The receptionist said the kidney-stent surgery cost $3,400 and payment was required in full and in advance. She cautioned that the dog would need aftercare—follow-up visits, MRIs, X-rays, and medication, possibly for the rest of his life. He could expect to spend up to $10,000.

Harry made an appointment for the following week.

He dug out the checkbook—Sally had always handled the money—and took out a pocket calculator that she had kept in the desk. He added up his Social Security money, veteran's benefits, and pension check. His IRA was almost gone. There was not enough there.

The dog was sleeping in his lap. Gus had been there for him. Now he had to be there for Gus.

Harry called his son, Richard, a state trooper in Colorado. He was levelheaded and smart, and he listened carefully to Harry's story.

"Dad, listen," he said, "I know you love the dog. But you

can't afford that kind of money, not now. And look, he's just a dog."

Harry thanked his son. His father would have said the same thing. The dog was just a dog, for chrissake. You had to have perspective. He had to think about his own future, be realistic.

Harry stepped out onto the patio—he loved the view out there, of the lake and the cypress trees. In Florida, he thought, everybody had a tiny slice of paradise, and on those breezy, sunny winter days, you really felt like you'd gotten away with something.

There was nothing Harry wanted that he didn't have. Except a longer life for Sally. And now, he wished that Gus would stay with him. How strange, he thought, to feel this way for a dog. Not something he would ever have imagined.

How could a strange-looking little pug with bulging black eyes and a grumpy disposition be anyone's angel?

But he believed it. Gus was watching over him.

Harry called the vet back. "I think we should put Gus down," he said. "I just don't have that kind of money. Can we make an appointment for Friday? That will give me some time with him."

The vet agreed and explained the euthanasia procedure—two shots, one to make him sleepy, one to stop his heart. He would feel no pain.

Harry felt a stab in his heart at the thought of Gus's eyes closing for the last time.

For just a moment, he felt a flash of rage. This was how it ended up? Unable to pay for a sick dog?

Harry sat with Gus on the patio. He didn't bark at passing dogs or cars. He didn't jump up and down. He didn't boss Harry around like he usually did.

THE NEXT MORNING, Harry got up early and made some oatmeal for Gus. He was happily surprised when Gus ate most of it. Maybe it was the splash of maple syrup—Gus was crazy about maple syrup. He heard a noise outside and woofed, and Harry wanted to cheer.

"You're a fighter, aren't you Gus?" he said.

He walked out onto the patio by himself. Gus followed slowly to the sliding glass door and looked out at him, wanting to come out.

Harry looked back at the dog, staring out at him. "I can't do it. I just can't. You're everything to me."

He went out to pick up the paper from the front lawn and brought it in. Then he took a pencil out of the desk where Sally had done the bills. Maybe that was the way life was. You were never really done fighting. Sometimes for your country. Sometimes for your family. Sometimes for yourself. Sometimes for your dog.

He called up the local paper. He said he wanted to place a classified ad, and he wanted it in the print as well as the online edition.

FOR SALE:
Motorboat: 74 HP engine, boat and engine good as new
Flat-screen HDTV
Patio set: table, four chairs, umbrella
Best offers
Items can be viewed Friday, 10 A.M., at yard sale.

He gave the address of his trailer park.

Friday morning, he put Gus on the bed and closed the door and turned on the air conditioner. Normally, Gus would have raised the dead at strangers coming up to the trailer, but this morning he barely moved.

About a dozen cars pulled in just before ten. Harry sold the boat and engine for $3,000. The flat-screen HDTV went for $800, and the patio set for $500.

He also sold an old rifle his granddaddy had given him, some of Sally's necklaces, a few books, an old boom box, a dozen Hummel figurines that Sally had collected, and a box of her Tupperware.

The sale was over in less than an hour. Harry collected the checks and drove over to the bank and deposited them. He called the vet to say he and Gus wouldn't be coming in that afternoon, then went to the hardware store and got a For Sale sign and put it up in his Dodge. He could make do with a smaller car. He didn't need that much space if it was just him and Gus.

Harry called the specialist in Fort Lauderdale to make an appointment.

On the morning of the surgery, Harry got up at four A.M. and drove with Gus to the clinic. It was a big, fancy place with lots of glass and high-class furniture.

The procedure was more complex than expected. The bill was nearly $7,000. He knew full payment was due after surgery. The sign said so.

Harry found a pay phone in the reception area. He called his son, who said, "I thought we'd agreed you wouldn't do this." But in the end, he agreed to put $500 on his credit card.

"Thank you, son." Harry gave him the number for the front desk so he could give the receptionist his information and hung up.

He called his brother back in Ohio, of whom he'd never

asked anything in his life, and his brother put $1,000 of the surgery on his credit card too.

Then he called one of his neighbors and told him he could have that fishing rod he always wanted, but it would cost him $350. He put that amount on his credit card.

Harry could see the receptionist was getting irritated as her phone kept lighting up. She mumbled something about feeling like a Walmart cashier, but Harry didn't care.

Finally, the receptionist said he had enough.

Harry nodded. *Wow,* he thought. *That was tougher than 'Nam.*

IT WAS SUMMER, and Harry spent most of his days indoors. The humidity was unbearable. Six months had passed since Harry had taken Gus to Fort Lauderdale. There were, in fact, two operations, and a later minor one. They had cost $9,000, all told. Harry had ended up selling the minivan for $11,000, so he had some left over for the after-surgery treatments and medications.

The operations were successful and Gus was himself again. Harry was leading a different life. He'd kept his trailer, but had given up his land line and now used a cell phone. The man who bought his big-screen TV heard about Gus and came back and sold the TV back to Harry on a monthly payment plan. Harry learned how to cook, to prowl around farmer's markets, collect coupons from the papers and at the market. Gus got fewer treats, and so did Harry.

Harry's arthritis acted up from time to time, and his walks with Gus were shorter and a little less frequent. But they both loved the big-screen TV.

In the afternoons, Harry would close the blinds and sit

down in the soft chair and talk to Sally, and tell her of the day that he and Gus had had.

Late one afternoon, when the brutal sun was losing some of its sting, Gus started barking. He was impatient, sitting by the door.

"Okay, okay," Harry said. He got up, put his big straw hat on, and opened the patio door. A blast of heat hit both of them dead on, but it didn't seem to bother Gus any. He raced out the back door, down to the dock, and into the boat.

Harry ambled along, pausing to get a Diet Coke and some crackers and biscuits. The new boat was a plastic dingy with a tiny Evinrude engine. It almost looked like one of those amusement-park boats that little kids rode around in.

Harry adjusted his straw hat and guided the little boat out to the middle of the lake. He looked at Gus's round belly. The surgical wounds had healed beautifully.

When he got to the center of the lake, he turned off the engine and sat back as the boat drifted. Gus barked at a pelican flying overhead.

"It's not your world only," said Harry. "Birds have a right to be here too."

Harry took out half of his peanut-butter-and-jelly sandwich. Gus focused on it, coming right up and sitting next to him with pleading eyes. Harry started eating it, but put a chunk of the other half on the floor of the boat. After a few minutes, both of them were licking peanut butter off the roofs of their mouths, making clicking sounds that drifted across the water. Harry threw a crumb over the side, and watched as a fish surfaced and grabbed it.

Gus looked up at Harry and wagged his tail. Then he barked at something on the shore. Harry smiled. It was the first time he'd smiled in months. Then he laughed out loud.

"Gus, you really are an angel," said Harry.

The wind died down, and the sun darted behind a cloud. The lake stilled. Harry felt himself dozing, slipping into a dream, as if finally beginning to let go of some of the pain and fear of the last couple of years. He felt as if he were walking through a field, shrouded in mist, and that Gus was looking up at him, the dog's eyes focused on his, his leash dangling on the ground. All his life he had summoned up his courage, done the right thing, kept his feelings and fears to himself, met his responsibilities. And now, it was as if all of those struggles were rolled into one, and he could see it, admit how hard it had sometimes been. Then he thought of his angel, and some of this was eased.

It's okay, Gus was saying. *It's okay, Harry, you can let go. You don't have to fight anymore. I have brought you this far. I'll take you the rest of the way.*

Dancing Dogs

KARA WENT TO THE HARRINGTONS' HOUSE TWICE A WEEK TO clean, dust, vacuum, take out the garbage, and brush the two imperious poodles who lived there.

Mrs. Harrington said it made her nervous to have people cleaning when she was home. But since she seldom left the house, there was little that Kara could do about the situation. Mrs. Harrington didn't like Kara making noise, moving things around, or interrupting her. If Kara had questions for her, she was supposed to leave them in writing on the kitchen table. Mrs. Harrington was especially prickly before her thrice-weekly card games. But Kara was paid well—$30 an hour—worth the hour each way she had to travel to the roomy old Victorian that was the Harrington home.

It was more than she got at Walmart, or at the 7-Eleven, or Target, or on the night shift at the factory in Argyle where she stuffed catheters into boxes and brought them to the shipping bay. It was more than the $10.50 she got at the supermarket, or the $12 she got driving part-time for the post office. And it was more than the $2.15, plus tips, she got waitressing at the diner on Route 40. The deal was the owner would make up the difference if the tips came to less than the minimum wage. This, she said, was the best joke since Brad told Jennifer they would spend their whole lives together.

Kara was a slight, wiry woman with brown hair cut short to keep it out of the way. Her husband, Greg, thought she worked obsessively, but then Greg had been out of work since the Clinton impeachment. At least he walked her three Welsh corgis every afternoon while she was out working, even though he and the dogs weren't crazy about one another.

Good jobs were not easy to find, especially for a small-town, upstate–New York girl with no college education, so even though Mrs. Harrington sometimes looked at Kara as though she were dog poop scraped off a shoe, it was regular work and she needed it.

One afternoon, Kara found that she was out of vacuum-cleaner bags. Unable to do her work, she momentarily forgot Mrs. Harrington's edicts, and walked to the doorway of the parlor, where Mrs. Harrington and her lady friends were finishing their delicate finger sandwiches before settling down to some bridge. Kara cleared her throat. Mrs. Harrington looked up, startled at the sound. The other three ladies hushed and clinked their spoons against their teacups, almost in unison. Mrs. Harrington's awful old cat, Martha, glowered at Kara and hopped up onto the sofa.

"Mrs. Harrington," she said. "Sorry to disturb you—"

Mrs. Harrington looked annoyed. She stood up. She didn't come over to talk to Kara privately or ask her what she wanted. Instead, she simply hissed across the room: "Kara, I've asked you not to disturb us during lunch. This better be an emergency."

Kara flushed. "There are no bags for the vacuum," she said, perhaps a bit more sharply than she intended.

Mrs. Harrington stiffened. "There's nothing I can do about that now, Kara. We're having lunch, as you perhaps can see. We'll deal with it later." And then she sat down. Kara was clearly dismissed.

She felt humiliated, standing there. She felt like a maid.

"Then I quit," Kara said. "If you can't deal with me cleaning your house, then I guess I can't either. I'll leave you to your lunch. I'll finish up, and then I'll be gone." And she turned, relishing the wide-eyed, open-mouthed stares of Mrs. Harrington's friends, and walked out.

Mrs. Harrington usually left her $60 in crisp new twenties. Kara took $40 and left $20. A tip, she thought, as she walked out the back door and drove her little Honda home to Greg and the three dogs—Ned, Sasha, and Candi—with their funny wide ears, docked tails, and low-to-the-ground waddles. Kara called them the Dancing Dogs—whenever she came home, all three rushed out to see her, squirming and barking and licking her fingers and legs.

When Greg came out to meet her, she smiled at him. Married nine years, and she loved him as much now as she had the day of the wedding. And the sex was still just as good.

He was holding a can of Bud, wearing his sleeveless sweatshirt and jeans, his feet were bare. The sedentary life was beginning to show in his belly now, which was starting to protrude.

"Hey," he said. "I found a candy wrapper on the floor of

the car yesterday. Didn't I ask you not to leave candy wrappers around?"

Kara looked up at the sky, as if imploring God to intervene. "Jeez," she said, "you get into the car with greasy hands and tools and leave stains all over the place, and you get on me about a candy wrapper?"

He shrugged. They had some version of this conversation at least two or three times a month, and they would probably have it until they died.

Since he'd gotten laid off from his factory job a little over a decade earlier, he hadn't pursued work too vigorously beyond the occasional glance at the classifieds, after which he uttered his ritual sigh and exclaimed, "Jeez, it's bad out there." Greg had been saying it was bad out there since long before the Great Recession, so for him, things really hadn't changed that much. What was the point of adding to those long lines? he asked.

He had a series of projects around the house—painting, woodwork, door trims—and around February, he always began serious preparations for deer-hunting season, which commenced in November. There was a lot to do, he often told Kara. Cleaning and oiling the guns, taking safety courses, practicing his tracking of the deer, scouting locations with his buddies, studying deer tracks in the mud and snow, and getting his license. And, of course, waiting for some perfect job to come along.

Maybe, Kara thought, a good job really will come along and hit you on the ass one day. But it had never happened to her. Somehow, Greg seemed to have quit on life, and that was harder for her to deal with than the loss of income.

She had also hoped for kids, but for medical reasons, that wasn't going to happen. And she blamed herself for that, and sometimes wondered if Greg didn't blame her too. But she did have her babies—they just had four legs instead of two. And they didn't whine or complain, think she was stupid, talk on their cell phones, or worse, plan to move out one day and get homes of their own.

"What are you doing home?" Greg asked, yawning. "Isn't it early? You didn't quit, did you?"

She told him what Mrs. Harrington had said.

Greg nodded sympathetically. "That bitch," he said. "Can't blame you."

The corgis were still doing their dancing thing, and Kara laughed. She clapped her hands and stomped a foot, and the corgis were all up on their hind legs, dancing around her in a circle, barking.

Greg laughed. "You ought to be in a circus act," he said, vanishing through the front door.

Greg liked to say that she liked him just fine, but she *loved* the dogs. Sometimes, she would take her boom box out in the yard on warm nights and get the dogs to dance with her. The neighbors loved the show, coming over with their kids to watch. The dogs danced in circles, jumping up and down, hopping back and forth. They danced in a row, in sync, like they were trained in Vegas. On command, the corgis would circle her and go up on their hind legs, spinning around while she tossed treats in the air. They especially loved to dance to Latin, country, and rock—music filled with percussion and fast tempos.

Pastor Steve had invited her and the dogs to a wedding reception at the church once, and they lit the place up dancing to a hyped-up version of "Amazing Grace" sung by Aretha Franklin. The dogs loved to dance to Aretha. The wedding family was delighted and gave her $50. She had thought then, Wouldn't this be a great way to make a living? Make money and have fun?

Kara went into the house to lie down. She put an ice pack on her head to quiet the migraine she felt rising up. She could have strangled Mrs. Harrington. Maybe Greg would finally get off his ass and find something.

She went out into the yard and Mrs. McKinney, the neighbor in the big Colonial next door, came over to talk. She loved watching Kara train the dogs, and while Kara was getting them to stand up and circle, Mrs. McKinney yelled over into her yard where her husband was trimming some hedges, "Hey, Charles, didn't you say the juggler for the Lions Club dinner tomorrow night got swine flu? Why don't you get Kara here to bring the dogs? They'd be wonderful." There was no response, but Kara saw Mr. McKinney watch the dogs for a while, concentrating.

The next morning, she went to the computer to check her e-mail. One popped right up: "Inquiring about Dancing Dogs. Urgent!"

She clicked to open it, and almost started to dance herself.

"Dear Kara," it read. "Regarding your Dancing Dogs and a possible appearance at our Annual Lions Club Members Dinner: As my wife mentioned, we had already booked a juggler. Yesterday, he was forced to cancel due to illness, and the dinner is tonight and we are in trouble. I have consulted with other members of the Lions Club Banquet Committee and we have a proposal for you.

"We have five hundred people coming for dinner at the Praetorian Inn near Schuylerville tonight. Are you available? I was impressed by the dogs yesterday. Can you advise me as to your fee? We had budgeted up to $1,000 for the juggling act. We can't really go higher than that. Thanks, your neighbor, Charles McKinney, Program Director, New York State Lions Club."

Kara fired off an e-mail. "Charles, as it happens, we have an opening in our schedule. We can make it, and $1,000 will be fine. Thanks, Kara and the dogs."

She included her phone number, and hit Send.

Then she panicked. What was she thinking, agreeing to a big show in front of the Lions? All sorts of people from the area would be there, and the dogs had no experience with a group that size.

Then she remembered the "Star-Spangled Banner" number that she had worked up, where the dogs danced in circles while the national anthem was played. That had brought tears to Greg's eyes when they'd practiced.

The phone rang. It was Charles McKinney.

"So, we're on?" he asked.

Kara gulped. She accepted. "I don't usually take gigs on such short notice. . . ."

Mr. McKinney added that he was on the board of the county fair and the Lion's Club had lunches and dinners all over the area, so there might be a chance for more business.

Kara put down the phone and screamed. Greg came running.

"We have a gig! A thousand bucks."

He grabbed her in a bear hug and spun her around.

She didn't have time for rehearsing. She had to drive forty miles to Schuylerville. She patched together a kind of outfit—it was the best she could do on short notice—red patent-leather pumps, a sequined miniskirt, a sleeveless blouse, and one of Greg's old cowboy hats.

She had six orange cones and some ramps she had

bought for an agility class she and the dogs had attended for a while. The cones and ramps and two hoops were the only props she had at this point.

She didn't know if the inn had a sound system, so she grabbed her boom box and two CDs—Shakira and Jencarlos's *Búscame*. She gathered up the three jeweled collars and stuffed them in a bag, along with a Ziploc bagful of kibble. She grabbed the box of liver treats and the leashes, then she rushed out to the Honda with the three dogs. Greg came out and gave her a kiss and a hug, and wished her luck.

An hour later, she pulled up to the inn and parked in the rear. When she and the dogs got out, a security guard came up and yelled that no dogs were allowed. When she told him they were part of the entertainment for the Lions, he looked dubious. He got on his walkie-talkie to check with someone inside, then waved her on.

Inside, she found Charles McKinney. They decided to keep the dogs in a storage room until dinner was nearly over and it was time for the entertainment. He led her down a hallway that ran alongside the big hall where the Lions were noisily working through their chicken dinners.

There was a kind of homemade stage in the front of the big banquet hall, raised up a bit in front of the scores of big round tables where all the Lions and their spouses and guests sat. The platform was a bit cramped—maybe fifteen by thirty feet, with a satin curtain in the rear and a backstage area. The dogs had not been on anything like it before, which worried Kara a bit. There was a sound system, so she handed McKinney her CDs.

"We appreciate your coming on such short notice," he said, adding that she would be paid after the performance.

He said the Lions' chorale would be singing on the stage after she and the dogs were through. She was a sort of warm-up act, he continued, smiling thinly.

"Thanks for the opportunity," she said.

McKinney quickly showed her the storeroom, and asked her if there was anything she needed, then left hurriedly to attend to other business.

There was a freezer in the back of the storeroom, the motor of which kept clicking on and off. Ned and Sasha seemed anxious. Ned walked over to a cardboard box marked "Napkins" and lifted his leg. She shouted at him to get off. Candi growled at the freezer. Then the overhead pipes started clanking, startling all four of them.

She could see her reflection on the side of the freezer. She looked a bit Vegas, she thought, in her short skirt and revealing blouse. She put the sequined collars on the dogs.

Fifteen minutes later, McKinney opened the door. "It's time to go on. I'll show you the way to the banquet hall."

Kara thought she was going to faint. She took a deep breath, took the dogs off leash, and jogged down the hall after McKinney. They waited outside while the announcer said the group was about to get a rare treat—a hot new act called "Tara and Her Dancing Dogs." Kara heard murmurs of approval and some clapping, and then at Mr. McKinney's cue, she opened the hallway door and charged in.

Onstage, she waited for the music. There wasn't any. She looked around the room at the two hundred or so Lions, many of them still working on dessert, waiters and waitresses scrambling around the tables. The lights in the room went down, and two spotlights hit her right in the face. She wasn't sure what to do until the music began.

The dogs looked at her expectantly, and she clapped her hands, reached for some treats and started to stomp her feet—the signal to the dogs that she was about to begin.

But the dogs didn't dance.

Suddenly, Ned and Sasha bolted off to her left, while Candi waited, staring at her treat bag.

She heard some guffaws from the audience. Then she heard a crash and bang offstage where two of her dogs had run. A few people booed. Worse, a few more laughed.

A stagehand appeared at the end of the platform, hissing at her and pointing to the rear. She called Candi over to her and yelled to the audience, "Wait a second, folks!" and ran off to the side. More laughing.

It seemed the dogs had startled a couple of stagehands carrying some chairs and a lectern, and these had fallen on the floor. Sasha was still sniffing madly toward the rear wall, while Ned was circling in confusion.

Kara clapped her hands and stomped, and the three dogs more or less gathered around her, except for Sasha, who had her nose down and was trying to get around the curtain. Kara looked out at the crowd and put her hands up, a signal to the dogs.

Suddenly, Shakira came blasting over a loudspeaker, and Candi and Ned hopped up on their hind legs, circling twice before there was another crash from backstage somewhere and both dogs took off out the door they had come in through.

Kara was beet red, the audience was chuckling and murmuring. McKinney appeared, sweating and uncomfortable. This was bad.

Kara bowed, fighting back tears, and called to Sasha.

"Hey!" she bellowed in a voice that could be heard distinctly from the back of the room. Sasha looked up and froze, as if she'd suddenly been awakened from a trance.

The dog hopped up on her two legs—Shakira was still blaring over the loudspeaker—and started dancing, although she seemed to be looking for the other dogs.

"Forget it," said Kara, and shooed the dog from the back of the stage and out the door, where they found Ned and Candi also hopping up and down and dancing to the music. Kara clapped her hands and led all three dogs back into the storeroom. McKinney followed her in.

"It's no big deal," he said. "These things happen." He gave her back her CDs and a check for $250 "for her trouble."

Kara was sobbing when she called Greg on her cell phone. "We made fools of ourselves because I put them in a position they weren't ready to deal with. I could just shoot myself. Now, nobody will hire us."

When she got back, Greg was on the phone. He was smiling. He even greeted the dogs. Something was up.

"I just called Old Man Frazier," he said. "He needs a driver to deliver mulch. He called me a month ago, but I blew him off. It pays fourteen an hour. Not great, but there's overtime if I want it."

Kara was speechless. This is not what she expected.

"But honey, driving a truck with mulch?" It wasn't what he had wanted. It was below his capabilities.

Greg walked over, put his arms around her, gave her a big hug and a provocative kiss, tongue and all.

"Kara, you need to make this thing with the dogs work. You've been cleaning houses and running cash registers while I've been sitting around, and now it's my turn to go to work and your turn to give what you want a shot. I'll help you."

Kara burst into tears. She hugged Greg, and patted him on his ass. He blushed. Enough said.

As it turned out, Greg actually liked his new job. In a couple of weeks, he was making enough money to cover the mortgage and most of their monthly bills, enough to give Kara some time to get her act together, he joked.

Kara decided to make the most of her chance. In exchange for maintaining the grounds and cleaning the clubhouse, a local Border Collie Association gave her morning use of their agility field, which had ramps, cones, hoops, and platforms.

Greg went off to work at seven A.M. But Kara was up at five, cleaning the house, doing chores, going online, reading her manuals and books. By sunup, she and the dogs were already at the agility course. She swept up the office, dusted, and emptied the trash bins. Then she went outside and cleaned up the dog poop, set up the cones, made sure all the bills and beams were set up properly.

After that, it was time to work. Dogs have short attention spans, so she decided to train in fifteen-minute intervals. She'd gotten chopped liver and raw hamburger and mixed the meat with a bit of molasses to make her own training treats. She'd also bought a rubber fishing pouch—the kind fishermen used to put their catch in—to hold the treats.

She tracked down two dancing-dog troupes in Florida, and they graciously spent hours on the phone with her, talking about routines and training methods, especially about how to keep the dogs focused on the work when there were so many unnerving distractions.

So Kara arranged for other dogs to appear suddenly, to bark and run around. Sometimes Greg came by in his mulch truck to bang metal drums and dance and yell to make noise. Other times, people came by with their intense border collies and Australian shepherds, and they ran through the agility course right in front of the corgis. Kara threw treats on the ground and made the corgis stay. She turned on her boom box and played sound-effect CDs with cheering crowds, traffic jams, thunder. All the while, she had them dancing through the mayhem. When they paid attention, they got the liver-burger-molasses balls. When they ran off, looked away, barked, growled, or acknowledged the parade of loud and raucous distractions, they got nothing. No treats, no praise. She would simply walk off the portable platform she and Greg had built as a practice stage.

She carved out a dozen fifteen-minute training periods, beginning at seven A.M. and working through to two P.M. She began each hour with a different dance or act. First, they hopped around to a Latin-beat selection. Then, they did a rock segment, where they jumped up and down to the Who and the Stones.

She worked on a "Born in the U.S.A." number, where the dogs raced in from offstage, jumped through three hoops, climbed to the top of a seesaw ramp, and did a kind of shake-'em-up corgi jitterbug.

There was one slow dance, where Ned and Candi sort of waltzed with each other to a Gershwin tune playing in the background. And then there was the Shakira finale, where all three dogs charged onstage and did a Rockette-style line dance. In between, they jumped through hoops, circled the agility cones, and then they danced in a circle around Kara while she raised her arms and did a cha-cha.

She eventually narrowed the acts down to three or four and concentrated on those, giving each a distinct name and musical background, and a different costume for her, so the dogs had plenty of cues.

KARA TALKED to neighbors, called schools and festivals, even tried to get an agent in New York City. No luck. One week, she put a small ad in the local *Pennysaver* offering her dog act for children's parties. A week later, she got a call from a woman named Jean Kashimian, a social worker.

Jean said she wanted to bring her to the Green Valley Nursing Home's Alzheimer's/Dementia Unit to perform for the patients there, many of whom were enrolled in the county's hospice program and were near death. Jean said Kara would have to present rabies-vaccination certificates, and they would put up a wire gate between the dogs and the patients at first, so there would be no potential for trouble. But the patients loved dogs, loved all kinds of animals.

Jean said they could pay $150 for a one-hour visit.

At first, Kara said she'd have to think about it. It wasn't exactly what she had in mind, but still, in the end, it was a gig, a chance to try out her training practices. She had to start somewhere. So she took the job after all.

One sunny, early winter day, she pulled up in her minivan to the sprawling, one-story nursing home. She had driven by it a thousand times, but never really looked at it before.

She took a deep breath, put the dogs on their triple harness, and let them out of the car. Jean was waiting in front of the main entrance.

"I can see you're nervous," she said. "Don't be. They'll love you guys."

Kara signed in and walked with her dogs down four long corridors. Kara could smell the institutional food right away, the potatoes and soup. When they got to a door at the end of a long hallway, Jean punched in a security code.

She explained that the code had to be used, as patients sometimes got confused or tried to get out. "They all think they're going home."

They walked into an atrium. The dogs' claws clicked on the smooth linoleum floors. Kara saw one elderly man strapped into a wheelchair shouting, "Martha! Martha! Martha!" over and over again. A woman next to him held her ears, and another was clutching her side in pain. Two women sitting on benches against one wall smiled and waved at her and the dogs. "Look, look, look!" said one, excited as a kid at a carnival.

Jean brought Kara and the dogs over to a small gated-off area that separated them from the patients. Immediately, one woman walked over and knelt to the floor. Candi came right up to her, waving her docked tail. The woman put her hands on her face and exclaimed, "Why, Spot! You used to be just a little poodle. And look at you now. You're a big brown and white dog with the most wonderful eyes."

Candi wiggled and squirmed with delight.

Another woman rolled up in a wheelchair. "This is my dog," she said. "I used to have this dog." She was smiling. Jean whispered to Kara that she hadn't spoken in months.

A man came up and looked angrily at Kara. "Are you ready to take me home? I'm waiting to go home."

No, she said, she wasn't. He cursed at her, and pointed his finger, until a nurse came up and gently guided him back to a bench.

Kara plugged in her boom box, and took out the Bruce Springsteen CD. When "Born in the U.S.A." came on, the dogs went up on their hind legs and danced for their lives.

The response from the audience was the strangest and most wonderful thing Kara had ever seen. People clapping, circling their wheelchairs, trying to dance with the dogs, yelling and shouting for joy. Afterward, Jean opened the gate, and the dogs rushed out to greet the patients, who leaned over to pet them and say hello.

One woman bent over so that she was almost nose to nose with Candi. "You remind me of my dog, you beautiful thing. My Hugo. I remember him." The nurse said later it was the first thing Mrs. McCandless had remembered in a long time.

"Nobody comes here, not even their families much," Jean said. "It means the world to them to see a dog. This is better than I'd hoped."

It took an hour for Kara and the dogs to get out. The corgis loved the attention.

Jean signed Kara and the dogs up for weekly visits to several nursing homes in the area. They said they could pay her $400 a month for five visits. Kara agreed.

Two weeks later, she got a call from a man named Harry Avanti. "I'm a local theatrical agent, from Albany," he said. "I don't handle Brad Pitt, but I have fun. I represent acts for weddings, county fairs, corporate meetings. My daughter-in-law, Jean Kashimian, always talks about the work you've been doing in the nursing homes. I've got a gig at the Columbia County Fair and one at the Washington County Fair. Your act is a natural. One thousand dollars for three performances over two days, two in the evening, one matinee. If this works out, I've got a dozen kids' parties coming up. I get fifteen percent, do all the bookings, and collect the money for you. What do you think?"

For once in her life, Kara was speechless. She couldn't believe it. She wanted to scream for joy, but just stood there opening and closing her mouth like a goldfish.

"Kara?"

"I'm just thinking," Kara said, trying to play it cool. "Okay, yes," she said. "Yes."

Lucky's Day

When Pete and Sally's alarm went off and they stirred in bed, the first part of Lucky's day began. He jumped up onto the bed to say good morning. Usually he got a cuddle, but today Pete and Sally were in a hurry, hopping out of bed and into the bathroom with just a cursory pat on Lucky's head.

Lucky was a small brown mutt with big ears and a short stumpy tail. The shelter people called him a "Heinz 57," as he seemed to be a little bit of everything. They told Pete and Sally that he might have been abused, which helped solidify the idea that the little dog needed to go home with them.

Pete and Sally did not believe in buying a dog when there were so many that needed homes. Lucky knew the word "abused." He heard it often, whenever he misbehaved, barked too much, growled at someone, peed on the floor, or looked particularly sad. Usually, those behaviors would result in more food and attention, so he began to think it was an important word.

Every morning while Pete and Sally got ready, Lucky lay at the foot of the bed, waiting for them to lead the way downstairs. For Lucky, going downstairs meant it would soon be time to have breakfast. But first, he was let out into the yard, while Pete or Sally yelled after him, "Good boy, Lucky, do your business!" which he did. As soon as he returned to the house, it was time to eat.

Some mornings, Pete or Sally would take him on a walk through the neighborhood, but that usually happened on days when they didn't have to leave. Lucky watched closely to see where they looked—if they looked at the coat rack, he would get a walk. If they didn't, he usually wouldn't. This morning, he didn't.

Lucky didn't know where Pete or Sally went, which made him anxious, as there was no way to keep an eye on them when they were gone. He often ran to the door, hoping to be taken along. A few times he raced past them and got as far as the car, but Pete or Sally always brought him back in.

"Get back, boy," said Pete, leaning over to stroke him.

"I always feel bad leaving him," Sally said almost every morning as she tossed a biscuit down on the floor to make Lucky feel better. "I bet he just mopes all day."

Lucky looked Pete in the eye, then Sally. As they moved to put on their coats, he whined and barked. "It's okay," said Sally, reaching down to pet him. "We'll be back."

Pete gave Lucky another treat to reassure him. But still, he looked stricken and Lucky knew it tore their hearts. As they headed for the garage, Lucky stared with a haunted look out the window. He whined and barked until they had gotten into the car and driven away.

ONCE THEY WERE GONE, the second part of Lucky's day began.

Pete and Sally went right out of Lucky's mind as soon as the car was out of sight. They simply vanished, and although he came across their smells all day, and certain things triggered images and memories of them, he would not otherwise think of them again until he heard the familiar sound of their car pull into the drive some time later. Lucky had no consciousness of what he could not see, no sense of the passing of time, no notion of the difference between one hour and one day. And he had a lot of other things to think about.

First off, he went into his crate, which Pete and Sally left open for him in the kitchen. He knew they didn't like to lock him up in it, but Lucky loved to spend time in there when he was alone. It gave him a sense of security and a chance to close his eyes for a few minutes, to orient himself to the quiet of the place. Sometimes he ducked into the crate when he heard sirens, which frightened him, or airplanes, which unnerved him. Or when other dogs or deer came too close to the house, and he had exhausted himself barking at them.

When Pete and Sally were gone, his notion of the house changed. It was quiet in one way, but the noises and creaks and other sounds were loud and continuous. Lucky left the crate and went to check the food bowl to make sure it was empty, then he continued on into the living room.

The house was two stories, but Lucky preferred only certain parts of it. He explored the house repeatedly, many times a day, and carefully. He was especially interested in the places with crumbs. And smells. People were messy creatures, scattering food, clothes, and other things everywhere.

Each day was a whole different story—varying smells of food, of Pete and Sally, of bugs and settling wood, and of shifting tiles on the roof. There was always something new to find, odors to follow. Lucky studied smells like a scholar, and never tired of them. Each morning, he painstakingly reviewed the scents of the previous day.

This day, he tracked pizza crumbs from the cracks of the tile near the oven, to the carpet underneath the dining-room table, where the pizza had been served, and in and around the sofa in the living room, where Pete and Sally had eaten. It was exciting work, and to do it properly and carefully took a good deal of time.

Then he hopped up onto the sofa that looked out onto the street, making it a good vantage point for keeping an eye on things. When Pete and Sally were in the house, he was usually not permitted on the sofas. They just didn't understand.

Lucky saw people in a nearby yard digging holes, and a dog sitting next to them. He growled and barked intermittently for half an hour. The dog turned to look at him but did not growl, or bother to challenge him. Mostly, the two just let it be known that each was aware of the other's presence. At first, Lucky's vocalization was a warning to stay away, but it soon eased into a sort of *Hey, how you doing?* thing.

When the other dog lost interest, Lucky jumped down from the sofa and patroled the living room, listening for the sound of the cat who always mysteriously appeared from upstairs. No sign of her yet.

Lucky's routine varied, depending on the weather. In

the summer, he sometimes went upstairs to lie on the floor of the tiled bathroom, which was the coolest spot in the house (and he could drink from the toilet bowl, which Pete and Sally didn't like but rarely saw). In winter, he liked Pete and Sally's bedroom, where he could jump up on the bed and stay warm (another place he was technically not permitted). Lucky also liked the vent in the living room, which blew hot air into the house, and was a good place to stay warm.

In the upstairs bathroom, he listened to the sounds of the water dripping through the pipes. He would tilt his head so that he could hear better, and puzzle over where the sounds came from and where they went. In this, he made no progress. But the familiarity of it was comforting to him. It was the sound of his house.

Back in the living room, Lucky took up his spot on the couch, where he could keep an eye on the neighborhood. Sasha, the cat, appeared, jumping up onto a sofa back and glaring at him. The cat mystified him; she ignored Pete and Sally most of the time and showed them little affection. She didn't seem nearly as skillful as he was in getting them to do things, yet they doted on her anyway. She spent considerable time in Sally's lap, and though Lucky was always seeking ways to drive her off, none were ever successful.

This morning when Sasha appeared, Lucky ignored her at first. Then he turned back to the cat for a Stare-Off, which usually lasted until Sasha either blinked or moved. This morning, she did neither, squinting at him through the narrow slits of her eyes. Lucky growled, which unnerved Sasha, and she hissed at him before hopping off the sofa, vanishing to some dark recess of the house. Sometimes, when there was a big storm or high wind, Sasha would appear and sit near

Lucky, and that was all right, as long as she didn't get too close.

When Lucky heard a scratching sound, he was off in a flash, moving up the stairs, and then toward the rear of the house and into the guest bedroom, a place he almost never visited. It was a warm, balmy day, and Sally had opened the window to let some air in. As Lucky turned the corner, he saw a squirrel sitting on the inside of the window ledge. Although Pete and Sally were never home to see it, the cheeky squirrels who lived in the big maples around the house often tried to get inside, especially in warm weather.

Lucky charged. The squirrel chirped in fright, then turned and darted out the window. Lucky threw himself up onto the bed and over to the window ledge, barking and snarling until the terrified squirrel disappeared into the tree outside.

Lucky waited a few minutes, and then trotted back downstairs. He felt an ancient, primal feeling of satisfaction and accomplishment. Several times a day, pigeons or other birds landed on ledges and gutters, and Lucky rushed up to bark and drive them off. The house was his to protect from human and animal intruders, and he was conscious of this at all times. It was intense work, and it went on all day.

The oil heater in the basement clicked on, then rumbled to life. Sasha streaked through the living room and disappeared again. Sometimes she went down into the basement, where Lucky rarely went. Pete and Sally left the basement door open a bit so that Sasha could go check for mice, but Lucky knew that Sasha didn't often chase mice. Mostly, the cat prowled the house looking for sunny spots to curl up in.

Often the mice came upstairs. If Lucky waited quietly in

the morning, after Pete and Sally left, he could hear their clicking and scratching in the floorboards on the far side of the kitchen.

When that happened, he was ready. He put his head low to the ground, and remained still.

Today, he watched the floorboards, and in a few minutes, he saw a tiny nose protrude through a small hole and sniff around. He understood mice well, even if the cat didn't. They never seemed to notice him if he remained still.

The mouse crept farther out, and then darted toward the area of the kitchen where the food was stored and where there were often crumbs. Lucky waited for him to get halfway across, and then charged. The mouse froze, then panicked, turning back and racing out through its hole. Lucky sniffed and barked and puffed himself up. More good work; well done.

Now, it was Listening Time. He returned to the crate.

Lucky raised his ears and closed his eyes. He lifted his nose to check for additional smells, some from the yard or farther, beyond the house. He heard mice moving in the basement—four of them, a family, skittering from one end of the dark space to the other, searching for food. He left them alone. He heard bees in a hive, in the eaves of the roof, and birds chirping in a nest in the big maple in the backyard.

He heard, then smelled, a dog walking with a human in front of the house. He ran to the front door and barked. The dog moved away. More good work.

He saw Sasha flit down into the basement and he heard the family of mice skitter through the spaces in the floor, hurrying to get outside the house.

He heard a snake slithering in the backyard, burrowing into the ground. The snake paused, then lunged at something and caught it. Lucky did not know what it was. He barked, and there was silence. He heard a mole digging near the garden.

He heard pigeons and songbirds talking to one another, flying overhead, landing in trees, building nests, feeding their young. He listened to their stories—of wind, flight, worms and other food, hawks and greedy crows.

From far off, he heard a dog, sending out a signal, barking insistently. Lucky was aware of every other dog in the area, and they were aware of him. He knew their barks and yips and whines and smells. The dogs of the neighborhood shared images, stories, and histories with one another. Pete and Sally and most other people would not have believed the things that Lucky knew and they didn't. Trapped in their own limited consciousness, people couldn't picture time spent in any way but theirs, nor imagine any language but their own. Yet Lucky talked to other dogs all the time, in his and their own way.

Lucky padded over to the sofa, put his paws up to the windowsill, and howled briefly. Instantly he heard a bark, got a story back, his head flooded with images. A retriever down the road had mated with a cocker spaniel from another neighborhood. It had been an accident—the retriever had gotten out and been drawn to a particular smell, and he found the spaniel in her backyard and hopped the fence. The humans were beside themselves.

Lucky relayed his driving off of the squirrel, and Sasha's cowardice in the face of mice.

The new rescue dog in the split-level at the end of the block reported confusion and astonishment over the behavior of the people who lived in the house. They gave him food, treats, toys, and invited him into bed. He didn't know how to respond. Lucky's advice was to look the humans in the eye, to act very excited when they came home, and to look mournful when they left.

People were busy, he said, and they gave many different commands in many different words. Something that upset them one day did not upset them another. It was the dog's job to be consistent, even when the people were not.

A Lab some distance away cautioned that while there was love between humans and dogs, there was also a kind of war. Everything that dogs loved to do—mating, fighting, eating dead things, rolling in dirt, foraging, marking their territory, digging in gardens—was forbidden by humans. The humans believed they were taking care of the dogs, but the dogs never quite grasped why they couldn't do the things that came naturally to them.

It was a trade-off, Lucky cautioned. You got food and shelter and attention, but you gave up much of your natural life as a dog. Most of time, it was a good deal. He counseled the new dog to accept this, not fight it.

Lucky added that it was important to train people, to condition them to offer treats. He was proud of his own ability, and had already passed the secret on to many dogs who appreciated it. "The Look" took weeks, even months, to perfect. It was a particular juxtaposition of the head and eyes that provoked a strong response in people—one in which they said "awww" or kneeled to the ground or took the dog's head in their hands and kissed his nose, or sometimes even cried. Lucky was not sure how it worked, but he knew it was a powerful trigger. Once the dog perfected it, he could pretty much do anything he wanted. And the Look often provoked the giving of food or attention.

There was a chorus of agreement. Look lovingly was the

other advice coming in. Love was important. The people seemed to need a lot of it, and they usually responded by giving something back—food, toys, walks. A basset hound said he was always anxious when the people left his house, but not in the way that they thought. He wasn't afraid to be alone, but they seemed to be starved for the kind of love that they got only from him. What happened to them during the day?

The bichon in the building in the middle of the block reported that he had nosed open the door of the boy who lived in his apartment. The boy kicked him often, and pulled his tail, so the bichon peed on his bed. Since the boy often peed in his bed himself, the people would be confused. The bichon would do it again. He also managed to get hold of one of the strange machines the boy attached to his ears all night, and he chewed it up and left it under the bed. When this happened before, the people seemed to blame the boy somehow, not him.

This prompted a chorus of cautions. Don't pee on the bed too often, or the people will figure it out. They were bad with smells, but good with some kinds of reasoning.

A Rottweiler-shepherd mix who lived near the park waited every day for the papers to come in through the slot in the front door, so he could tear them up to prevent them from entering the house. One of the games he played with the people in his house was the number of ways they tried to block the door—chairs, wire, boxes, odors that were meant to deter him, even an electric wire that shocked. But he understood the game, and played it well. He was able to handle the shock, chew through the wires, push aside the door, and tear the paper into bits, and he received enormous amounts of attention for this when the people came home—they yelled at him, grabbed him, shouted at him. It was great fun and he loved the game.

A Labradoodle got into a fight in the dog run and was injured slightly—a tear in the ear. The humans were very upset and began fighting with the people who owned the other dog. Fighting among dogs seemed to anger and frighten them, a difficult thing for all of the dogs to understand. It was one of the ways they communicated with one another, sorted things out in the hierarchy.

A mutt reported triumphantly that he had managed to nip the heels of a man who invaded his front sidewalk every day wearing a red shirt, shorts, and white shoes, running past the house clearly to provoke the dog, who waited for months until a window was open, and then jumped out and pursued his prey. He got him on the leg, and the man shouted and kicked at him. Later, the people he lived with yelled and shouted at him also; and then they built a new fence, although he had no notion of why.

A border collie near Lucky told the strange story of his life, how he was brought from a farm to this small house with nothing to do, so he busied himself by digging holes under the fence and chewing through the latch to keep from going crazy. The people had put a collar on him that shocked him whenever he came near the fence. But he had plans to escape. Other dogs were familiar with the collars and fences, and one said it was sometimes possible to run through the latter. The border collie said he might run through his fence and try to find his old farm.

The dogs grumbled and gossiped with one another, sharing stories and news of their lives, of families and weather, of food and garbage, of the neighborhood and of their struggles to acclimate themselves to the intensifying needs of humans. The old-timers told stories of difficult and violent times. The Labs told tales of meals and food, and the border collies chattered on about work they needed to do, and things they needed to explore. The mutts and rescue dogs talked of their time in the shelters and of their new lives in new places.

But they always got back to the humans, the people who shaped and controlled their lives, on whom they were so dependent. The strange ways they communicated, their impatience, the ways to reach them and get food and attention from them.

People had difficulty leaving dogs behind. Their lives away from the dogs must be empty and boring. Lucky felt bad about the people being alone all day.

Some of the dogs had different notions about this. It was tiring to be at home all day, there was so much to do: cats to monitor, birds and mice to listen for, people to chase away from the house, sirens and engine sounds to bark at, and other dogs to listen for and talk to. It was a relief at night when the people came home. Only then was it possible to sit around and sleep.

A shepherd down the street barked mournfully, and Lucky tilted his ears to listen. It sounded important. Dogs were individualistic and selfish, he knew, but the shepherd was unusual in that he spoke about other dogs, and seemed to have a larger view of their lives beyond the confines of a single house or yard. He told Lucky and the other dogs that the lives of dogs were changing. They lived their own lives, in their own places, and the old ways of the packs were dying. Dogs no longer took care of themselves, lived in dens, or hunted together. Understanding people was everything. There was great loss in this, he said.

When Lucky heard the old shepherd talk, it stirred things inside of him. It was true, some of what the old dog said. He had never run free outside, or mated, or walked without a leash. He had always lived in an environment with narrow boundaries—the house, the street, the park—but within it, he'd created his own sense of the world. He enjoyed his day, his time with Pete and Sally, and his secret life in the house.

Lucky thought his people must be mistreated during the time they were away, as they seemed so sluggish and sad to him when they returned. The dogs were all mystified that the people they lived with had all kinds of food around, closed up in boxes and cabinets, and they only ate it two or three times a day. And they eliminated in small rooms, out of sight of one another. And they only slept in certain places, and usually only at night. And they had no notion of waiting, and were rarely ever still or at peace.

Just then, a dog a mile away signaled the daily warning. The blue and white truck was coming. The dog was trying to drive it off. These signals went out all day. There were blue and white trucks, blue and red trucks, brown trucks, big noisy trucks that picked up trash and banged metal cans, trucks that howled with lights that flashed.

They all had to be made to go away. They had to keep the houses safe.

Lucky raised his head. He heard the blue and white truck turn onto the street, and then it was quiet. It came almost every day.

He heard the man with the bag get out and begin walking from house to house, bringing things to a box out front, or pushing packets of paper through slots in the front door.

Lucky barked, charged to the door, turned in circles,

made as much noise as he could. Success! The man went away. Every day Lucky accomplished this; in fact, it was his most continuous and important success. He was proud of himself that when he barked and growled, the strange man vanished. The man had never once made it into the house.

But this left Lucky tired, so he returned to his crate, and nodded off to sleep.

As the light began to fail, he realized he was hungry. The other dogs had quieted, going about their own business. He took up his position on the sofa, looking out the window and keeping watch. Sasha appeared on the other side of the room and settled onto one of the chairs.

From far away, he heard the engine of Pete and Sally's car. He jumped off the sofa, and took up his post by the back door.

Lucky heard barks and signals from all over the neighborhood as the people began returning. There would soon be food. Treats, walks, balls, visits to parks, other dogs, other people.

He heard the car pull into the driveway, next to the garage. He heard the sound of footsteps.

"Oh, Lucky! Poor baby! Alone all day!"

Puppy Commando

HELEN WOULD HAVE LOVED THE ANNUAL SCHOOL FIELD TRIPS TO the local animal shelter if she could have taken home a puppy—which she had coveted almost every conscious day of her twelve years on earth—but her parents wouldn't allow it. It was torture to visit dogs and cats that needed homes and know that you wouldn't be taking one with you. She'd heard every possible excuse for why they couldn't have a dog: Her mom might have allergies; her dad wasn't really a dog person; they were busy and away from home too much; their neighbors might object; dogs were too expensive; they dug holes in the garden; they shed fur everywhere; they chewed everything from shoes to table legs; they ate garbage; they rolled in stinky things; they barked; they slobbered; they drooled. Mostly, she thought, her parents just didn't believe that Helen was responsible enough to take care of a dog.

They were wrong, but Helen doubted she'd ever have a chance to prove it.

Mrs. Wuraftic, her seventh-grade social-sciences teacher, urged the kids off the bus, through the parking lot, and into the shelter's lobby, where a worker wearing a badge began talking to them about the shelter—who paid for it, where they got the animals, how the adoption process worked. Helen tried to listen but she was distracted by the barking dogs, each of whom seemed to beg to come home with her.

HELEN WAS THE OFFICIAL CLASS ODDBALL, though the other girls had called her meaner names than that. Over time, she had learned, as many girls do, to make sure nobody knew what she was really like, to hide those parts of herself that were most vulnerable. But rather than pretending to be interested in the newest teen hunk or fruit-flavored lip gloss, she wore an exaggerated form of her individuality like armor, protecting herself with the very same eccentricities that betrayed and isolated her.

She didn't notice what the other girls were wearing, nor did she giggle or moon over boys. She did not tweet about the inane details of her life or post intimate photos and experiences on Facebook. In the age of continuous connectivity, Helen was simply not connected. She browsed the Internet and researched her homework there, just like the other kids, but she was allergic to the social media that consumed her peers. For them, there was no part of life that was not known or shared.

Helen was an only child and not well constituted for the social complexities and politics of middle school. She pined for friends, but didn't quite know how to make them. Animals were the only living things—other than her kind but somewhat distant parents—who didn't make fun of her. She had always loved animals. And she wanted a puppy desperately. She needed one.

Iris, her preassigned "buddy" for the trip, was one of the popular girls. She rarely deigned to look at Helen, let alone talk to her, but she was clearly excited to be at the animal shelter. "I can't wait to see the dogs and cats," she said, craning her neck around the cluster of their classmates. "I love animals. We've always had dogs, and I really, *really* want a cat."

Helen felt the same way about animals, but she didn't have any, and she wasn't prone to gushing. "I just hope we get to see some puppies," she said, popping one of the cheese crackers she always kept in her pocket into her mouth.

It was time for them to head into the shelter. "Remember," Mrs. Wuraftic told them, "no talking. Walk in a single file. Don't touch any animals. Stay together."

JULIUS WAS LONELY. He and his siblings had been found in the basement of an abandoned house and brought into the shelter. The healthy ones had already been adopted and the really sick ones had been put to sleep; he was the last of his litter and was isolated in a special room in the shelter. People streamed by all day to look at the other dogs and cats, but they never came into the room where he sat in his crate, listening for them and waiting.

The day before, he had been knocked out. When he woke up, his leg, which hurt badly, was in a large white cast and he could barely move. He howled and yelped for his mother, his brothers and sisters—for anybody or anything. But the shelter workers came in only twice a day to hold him, feed him, give him medicines, and move his leg around, which hurt.

This morning Julius was alert, focused on the window of the sickroom where he knew people would pass by. He was eager to move beyond the small space and out into the world, to a calling he was drawn to but could not quite picture. It was a need, an instinct, perhaps his strongest one.

These people were shorter than usual, and most of them walked right by the room where his crate was kept. He raised his nose in the air and caught a scent. It was a girl, one who smelled just a bit like cheese.

Julius did not think like a human. He didn't have organized thoughts, just images and smells that came pouring into his mind. The face of a young girl. A sense of need, of loneliness. A connection. He felt something ancient and inherited stirring inside of him, drawing him to this girl who evoked just the right mix of needs and feelings. She was his person, and he knew it with every fiber of his damaged body. Something deep inside of him awakened, and he howled and howled at the top of his very young voice.

IN THE HALLWAY, Helen found it easier to talk to Iris than she had expected. The two really did share an interest in animals, and they "awwwwed" and exclaimed over a golden retriever puppy, three newborn kittens, and a Great Dane with enormous brown eyes. Helen saw that Iris's love of animals was real, not just an affectation. She suspected that the class social butterfly was both bright and nice underneath the elaborate and sneering social veneer she had constructed to make herself popular. Maybe, just maybe, they could spend more time together.

Helen heard a faint but piercing howl and turned toward the sound. She peered through the glass window on a door marked No Admittance—Medical Procedures. The howl was insistent, distinctive, and she had a strong reaction to it. Somehow, she knew—*knew*—it was meant for her.

"Listen to that dog! I've got to get in there," Helen told Iris, who was chewing her ever-present bubble gum and glancing down at her cell to see if anyone had texted her since they'd left the lobby.

"You're not allowed—it says 'No Admittance,'" said Iris, her usual scorn for Helen returning.

Helen was a bit surprised. She thought Iris might understand how she felt, how drawn she was to the sound, but the popular girl backed away and joined a cluster of her friends farther up the line. I should have known better, Helen thought.

"I don't care," she said aloud. "I'm going in."

As Mrs. Wuraftic and the shelter workers led her classmates into the adoption bay, Helen, her heart pounding with excitement, grabbed the door and stepped into the darkened room. It felt a little creepy in there, and the second the door clicked behind her, she worried she had made a mistake. She couldn't see much of anything, but she heard some whining and stirring and rustling. When she turned toward the sounds, she saw a tiny pair of brown eyes that shone faintly in the light coming from the hallway. Those eyes seemed to bore right into her soul, as if they knew her. As if they were saying, *Helen, where have you been? I've been waiting so long for you.*

But the door opened suddenly and Mrs. Wuraftic's voice came rocketing into the quiet room: "Helen! What are you doing in here? Do you want to get detention? Get out of here right now."

Mrs. Wuraftic's steel grip closed on Helen's arm, and her

teacher pulled her out into the hallway. Iris and her friends were giggling and sneering at Helen. She fantasized about sticking a wad of gum to the back of Iris's sweater, but she knew she couldn't do it. Helen did not really understand cruelty, except that she was often on the receiving end of it.

Mrs. Wuraftic took Helen out of the shelter and told her to stay on the bus. A note would go home to Helen's parents, who would be surprised. She didn't break many rules and almost never got into trouble. She would just tell them she got confused.

IN JULIUS'S ROOM, the smell of the young girl—and the cheese—had gone away. But she had still been imprinted on his consciousness, and she was, now and forever, his person—the person he was meant to be with and love. He was just a baby, but he already had the full instincts of a dog. There had been a moment, a connection. And now, he couldn't forget the girl, even if he'd wanted to. Where had she gone? He had sensed her frustration, anger, and sorrow. And he knew she'd felt the connection too. He raised his nose again and again to find her smell. But it wasn't there.

Julius whined and howled for the girl, first softly, then loudly, but his keening cries only brought a few shelter workers in to check on him. They gathered around him and spoke in soothing tones, but Julius would not be consoled. He could not possibly make them understand.

THAT NIGHT AT DINNER, Helen, a poor liar, told her parents the truth. She said she'd heard a dog howling and felt a connection. "That's my dog in there, my puppy, and I think he's sick. We need each other." She explained that she looked for him in the Medical Procedures room. And she told her surprised parents—Helen rarely asked for anything, let alone demanded anything—that she was going to go back to the shelter to see about adopting him.

"It was an amazing moment," she told them. "I don't know, we just connected. I'm old enough to have a puppy and take care of him." Her father began reciting the familiar list of reasons why Helen couldn't get a dog, but she put her hands over her ears and stormed off to her room. This time, she refused to hear it. Her parents looked at each other in confusion.

"I've never seen her like this," her father said in bewilderment.

"She's never *been* like this," said her mother, equally dumbfounded.

HELEN HAD ALWAYS WANTED a puppy not only because they were adorable, but because she and the dog could grow up together. She already knew she would need that; she could barely speak to her peers. But now, she no longer just pined for any dog. She pined for the dog that had howled for her at the shelter.

Later, when she went downstairs for a glass of water, her mother was sitting on the sofa as if she'd been waiting for her.

"Helen, we should talk."

"No, Mom," said Helen. "We talk all the time. We should go to the shelter together after school and look for this puppy. I love you and Dad, but you don't understand how difficult my life is. I need this. Badly."

THE NEXT AFTERNOON, Helen and her mother arrived at the shelter. Since Helen was a minor, she couldn't adopt a pet by herself, but her mother let Helen do the talking. She was surprised by her daughter's poise and determination. She hadn't seen that in her before.

Helen explained that she had gone into the Medical Procedures room by mistake. Was the puppy crated in that room up for adoption?

"That's Julius, a nine-week-old beagle," said the adoption counselor, her ID badge clinking against her necklace. She looked sad. "I'm very sorry to tell you that he's not up for adoption. He was injured—we think he was hit by a car or motorcycle—and his right hind leg was shattered. He had surgery yesterday and he will be in a cast for weeks."

Helen met the women's gaze and fought back tears. "Why isn't he up for adoption then?"

The woman looked over at Helen's mother before answering. "Well, we don't know if he'll get through this, and if he does, he'll need a lot of care. We don't put sick dogs up for adoption. No exceptions."

There was a long silence in the room. Helen finally burst into tears, and her mother took her hand and started to lead her out of the adoption room and toward the main lobby.

Suddenly, all three of them heard a mournful howl, more piercing than loud. It cut right through the din of the other dogs and cats.

Helen whipped her head around. "That's him!" she exclaimed. "That's him. I need to see him." The shelter director looked at Helen's mom and shook her head. And so Helen's mother took her arm and guided her out of the shelter.

JULIUS SMELLED THE GIRL and recognized her voice. She was in the shelter again. His howls had brought her back. He waited for her to come to him, and when she didn't, he took a deep breath, lifted his head to the skies, and let out the loudest howl a puppy could produce.

And then she was gone again. He'd lost her smell. Julius whined and howled all night. He didn't eat any of his food. No one at the shelter could console him, or figure out why he was so upset.

THE NEXT MORNING Helen woke up at six A.M., left a note for her mother explaining that she had gone to school early, and walked two blocks to the bus stop. The 114, which cost $2, went right by the shelter.

When she arrived at seven A.M., it wasn't yet open. She walked around to the back and looked around, then took off her backpack and hid it behind the big green Dumpster.

She used the rear loading dock to get into the shelter and was met by a security guard sitting at a desk by the back door, drinking coffee and playing a game on his cell phone.

"Can I help you, miss?" asked the guard suspiciously.

Helen blushed, stammered, then recovered. "I'm a volunteer—a junior volunteer," she said quickly. "Our class came by earlier this week, and I volunteered to come in the mornings and help socialize the animals. You know, take them out for walks, sit with them, and stuff."

The guard looked around. "You here alone?"

"Yes, my mom dropped me off on her way to work," she said, marveling at the lies that kept slipping out of her mouth.

The guard looked wistfully at his muffin and coffee, then picked up the phone and spoke quietly before hanging up.

"I talked with the night staff, and they don't know about any volunteers," he reported. "I can't let you in here on your say-so, miss. Besides, the dog you're here to see is leaving the shelter today. I know you were here the other day."

The look of grief and shock on Helen's face was so powerful and genuine that the guard's expression changed quickly from one of wariness to sympathy.

"They told me he was going off to a vet school, where they would know how to work on his broken leg," he told her.

Helen nodded, wiping the tears from her eyes. "Can I see him?" she asked. "Just to say good-bye? I know he's in the Medical Procedures room, 'cause that's where I saw him when I first came to volunteer."

The guard looked up at the clock, then at her. "I don't see why not," he said carefully, "but you can't go in now, not without an escort. You can come back when we're officially open and there are more staffers here. I can't let you wander around the shelter alone. If you get lost or one of the dogs bites you, I'll be out of a job. You don't want that, do you?"

Helen said no. She thanked the guard and headed out of sight toward the bus stop. Then she circled back and listened by the door. In a minute or two, she heard a chair scrape, and then she opened the door a crack. The guard was gone, perhaps to the bathroom. She crept in quietly and closed the door behind her.

JULIUS SMELLED THE girl the minute she came into the shelter. He smelled the cheese crackers also. His barking had worked again. He was a social creature and liked humans, but he had attached to this one in a new and particular way. It would be for life. There would not be another connected to him in this way, and he knew it in his bones.

He could hear her talking to another person, an older one with a deeper voice. The girl sounded sad to him, and lonely. He stood up in his crate and started making a racket. He longed for this girl whom he could sense and smell but not quite picture.

He missed her.

THE DOOR TO JULIUS'S CRATE opened. "Poor thing," said an unfamiliar human voice. "He can't run or walk much. I'll put him in the bigger open pen where he can move around a little bit. He'll be confined in the van for a long time."

Two hands came in and gently lifted him out. He was given a pungent treat, carried down the hall, and then placed on the floor in a large pen with sawdust on the bottom and the smells of many other animals, mostly dogs. He could only move slowly and it hurt, but he began to sniff, soaking up the stories in the smells of the place. There were a lot of sad and painful stories in that pen, and Julius trembled. He took small and careful steps before coming to the door at the end of the pen. He howled for the girl.

• • •

HELEN THOUGHT SHE HEARD her puppy. She found the Medical Procedures room and opened the door. It was dark inside. She dropped to her hands and knees and crawled to his crate. But there was no dog inside it. He was gone.

An envelope taped to the front of his crate read "Pennsylvania Regional Veterinary School, Research Lab." She tore open the envelope and read the note inside: "Julius . . . male beagle . . . nine weeks . . . multiple leg fractures . . . picked up for surgery, rehabilitation, tensile-tendon experimentation, and, if possible, eventual re-homing."

Helen didn't understand the word "re-homing," but what really bothered her was "experimentation." Her mind raced. Was the vet school going to experiment on him? She had heard about labs where they practiced complicated surgeries on dogs and cats without homes. Animal-rights groups were always protesting these experiments, but the vets argued that there was no other way for them to hone their surgical skills and learn about the insides of animals. How else would they get to practice? She didn't know, but practicing on a live animal didn't seem right to her.

She opened another crate and picked up a happy, squirming black puppy, a small girl. She cuddled it then put it back. It was adorable, but she didn't feel the same thing she felt with the injured beagle. She didn't know why. Her father always said that one dog was like another, but she didn't agree. And this puppy didn't howl.

People were starting to come into work, and she had to get out of there—she couldn't just wander around the place looking for Julius. She opened the door a crack, peered into the hallway, and ran back the way she came. The security desk was still vacant. She rushed out the back door and into the parking lot.

POWERED BY SOMETHING INSIDE of him, something beyond his consciousness, Julius stuck his nose in the door latch, which had been left open from the outside. He did not howl. He simply pushed at it, and pushed again, then squeezed his thin frame through the narrow opening, dragging his sore and awkward leg behind him. Although his leg hurt, the puppy had no real concept of pain. He couldn't really remember ever not feeling it, and so it seemed almost natural to him.

There were no people in the room, and the door to the hallway was open. He passed other dogs in cages, some friendly, some not, and some cats who hissed at him. His movement touched off a din in the room, and he limped to the hallway as quickly as he could. There he picked up the smell of the girl and began to follow it, his tail wagging excitedly. He was a nose dog. It was time to get to work. He picked up another smell—cheese again—and moved even more quickly.

Julius just kept moving toward her smell, dragging his cast behind him. He never stopped or slowed down, not even to investigate all of the rich scents that swirled around him and told him so many other stories.

HELEN WAS PANICKED. Her mother knew she was not at home, and her teachers would soon know she was not in school. She had no permission to be out on her own, and she knew her parents would be anxious about her. They might even call the police if they thought she was missing or had run off. Which, in a way, she had.

And she had an awful feeling that she was too late for Julius—that he had already been shipped off to a vet hospital where he would face a life of experimental surgery and never know the love of a home. Or of her.

Tears streaming down her cheeks, she ran through the parking lot and toward the Dumpster to get her backpack. When she rounded the corner, she froze. There, his cast sticking awkwardly out to the side, sat Julius, right on top of her backpack. When he saw her, his tail started going a mile a minute and his piercing yowl cranked up in joy.

Helen broke into a run and grabbed the dog. "Shh! I can't believe you're here! But you have to be quiet or they'll hear us." Julius's howl quieted to a whine, but his tail continued to move like a helicopter blade. She hugged him, supporting his cast carefully, while Julius licked the tears from her cheeks. She smelled cheese and saw some crumbs dropping from his mouth—he had found her stash of crackers in the backpack. She could hardly believe how soft he felt, how sweet his puppy smell was.

"My boy, my boy," Helen whispered softly. She picked up a stick and punched a hole through the bottom of her backpack. She carefully placed the squirming puppy inside. Julius fit perfectly, his leg cast sticking through the hole at the bottom and his head poking out of the top. She put the pack on backward so that Julius hung off her chest, where he could see her and look over her shoulder at the world. It seemed like he had been born to this, being carried by Helen.

But she was terrified. Helen had never skipped school without permission, lied about anything major, or stolen anything in her short life, and in just a couple of hours, she had done all three.

She peered out from behind the Dumpster. Then she looked down at Julius. He was where he belonged, finally. He was a happy puppy, one of those dogs who would go anywhere with the person he loved, trusting and content.

Helen wished she felt the same.

She heard some shouts coming from inside the shelter. They must be looking for Julius, and perhaps for her. The guard may have told them about her, or her mother might have called. Even the school.

But she was not giving up. This was her puppy. It was meant to be. Helen leaned forward and kissed him on the nose. "Let's go, boy," she whispered, and started running along the far side of the parking lot, shielded by trees and cars. At the edge of the lot, she knelt behind a hedge and made sure that the shelter workers hadn't seen her. When she felt safe, she rose to a crouch and ran down an alley behind some houses.

She would go a half block, and then she would hide. She hid in an open garage, behind an appliance store, in the shadow of a fountain in the park. Twice, Helen stopped and took Julius gingerly out of the backpack to let him pee, and then they cuddled for a bit before she put him back in. He seemed tired, and she wondered if he needed some medicine. Maybe she had been foolish to take him away from his doctors. Maybe she had put him in danger.

She was getting tired herself. When she was only a few blocks from home, she let her guard down. She walked out in the open, still carrying her puppy on her chest. Julius was asleep now, his head drooping down over the backpack.

Just as she turned onto her street, she heard tires scream and saw flashing red and blue lights.

"Young lady, stop right there!"

Helen froze when she heard the police officer's voice. She was a criminal, and she didn't want to get shot. She didn't want Julius to get shot either.

But the police officer was surprisingly calm and nice. He didn't do any of the things police officers did on TV. He got out of the car, introduced himself as Officer Jenkins, and asked if she was the little girl named Helen who had taken a dog out of the county shelter. She nodded, tears running down her cheeks, and she nodded again when he asked softly if this might be the dog.

He asked if she would like a ride home, and she bobbed her head. "No handcuffs, I guess," he said.

It was the strangest and most embarrassing ride of her life. Her face was beet red, and she lowered her head to avoid the stares of neighbors and kids riding their bicycles on the street. The dog curled up in her lap and trembled—he was clearly not used to riding in cars. She reached in her pocket and took out a cheese cracker, ate half and gave the other half to the puppy.

When the police car pulled into the driveway, Helen's mother rushed out of the house and hugged her until she thought her neck might break. She introduced her mother to Julius, and although her face softened when she saw the puppy, she still looked Helen in the eye and said, "You know this dog doesn't belong to you. You do know that, don't you?"

Helen nodded, too choked up to talk, but she wouldn't let anyone else hold Julius.

Her father was there too, having rushed home from

work when he found out she was missing. He took her onto the porch while she clutched the puppy. "Helen, I want to say something to you," he said. "What you did this morning was wrong, and I'm thinking of ways to punish you. But I understand why you did it, and even though I'm angry, I'm also proud of you for being so brave. I love you, and I've realized that I don't really know my little girl as well as I should. I'm going to fix that." And then he gave her—and Julius—a big hug.

Her parents drove her to the shelter, and Officer Jenkins followed them there. Helen wouldn't let Julius out of her grip, but once there, she allowed Dr. Jaffe from the Pennsylvania Regional Veterinary School to examine him, check his cast, and give him some medicine for the pain. The puppy seemed to be greatly enjoying all of the attention, but he never took his eyes off Helen. If anyone tried to take him away from her, he yowled so loudly that everybody in the room would wince.

The shelter director explained that Julius was not up for adoption because he wasn't strong enough. "He needs surgery and a lot of care, and we don't want any family to take home an unhealthy animal. It's our responsibility to take care of him until he's healed. If he survives the necessary surgery, he'll be put up for adoption then."

Dr. Jaffe told her that the vet school provided expensive surgeries to shelter animals for free. And then they returned them. The school did not experiment on dogs or cats. Students at the vet school would operate on Julius's leg—under the strict supervision of their teachers—and then return him to the shelter. If Helen wished to adopt him then, she could. Dr. Jaffe looked at Julius and Helen and smiled. "Seems like a good fit."

The shelter director said it was wrong for Helen to have stolen Julius from the shelter. Imagine if a person had been bitten. What if Julius had hurt his leg further, and needed attention? Sick animals needed care, and they could be dangerous.

Helen nodded her head as she considered the director's words. She hadn't thought about Julius hurting anyone, but she had worried that she'd put the puppy in danger.

"I'm sorry for stealing Julius," she said seriously, "but I didn't actually take him out of the shelter, honest. I was planning to, but he wasn't in his crate so I left. He got out by himself, and I found him sitting on my backpack behind the Dumpster."

The director raised her eyebrows. "I have a hard time imagining this injured puppy escaping from an enclosure, getting out of the shelter, and walking across the parking lot unaided and unobserved," she said. "I'm not saying I don't believe you, Helen, but it's a stretch."

Helen could see that the director clearly did *not* believe her. She didn't know what to say. It *was* a stretch. "It's the truth," she said, her eyes welling up a bit.

"Okay," the director said, "if that's what you say." She paused for a moment, studying Helen, then continued. "If the operation goes well, and I hope it will, you'll be welcome to apply to adopt Julius. But I can't promise anything. We'll have to consider what's best for the dog. And your entire family must be on board."

Officer Jenkins stood up and leaned over to kiss Julius on the nose. "For what it's worth," he said, "I'm around a lot of people who lie well, and Helen here, I don't think she knows how." Helen blushed and smiled shyly.

Then he shook her hand, said he had other more serious

criminals to attend to, and wished her luck. "Don't be running away from home or stealing anymore dogs, young lady," he said, and winked. "Next time, I'll use the handcuffs."

"Thanks for the ride, Officer," she said, looking him in the eye. He smiled.

Helen was surprised at how nice the vet and the shelter director were, all things considered. She was sorry that she had stolen Julius. But not very. Not really. She loved him now more than ever, and she was worried about the surgery and whether her parents would let her adopt Julius if he made it through. And she was very tired.

THREE WEEKS LATER, Julius came home. Helen's parents had gone to the shelter, filled out the adoption papers, and paid the fee—$75—which would come out of her allowance as punishment for cutting school, leaving home without permission, and stealing the dog from the shelter. Helen also agreed to volunteer at the shelter twice a week, cleaning up the messes in the dog and cat crates. She was happy to do it.

The vet techs from the hospital lifted Julius's crate out of the van and put it on the sidewalk, and Helen, who heard the yowling from inside the house, came running out to open the crate and pick up her puppy. They had fought long and hard to be together, and now, they finally were. Maybe it was true, Helen thought. Maybe if you wanted something badly enough, it might actually happen.

Julius had steel pins in his knee and would always walk with a bit of a limp, the doctors at the vet school told her, but he would be fine. He could go for walks, chase balls, sniff things, and easily climb the stairs to get to Helen's bedroom, where he would sleep for the rest of his days. She would have to watch out for arthritis when he got older. And she'd have to monitor his medications and learn how to massage his leg and give him physical therapy.

But none of that mattered. Helen was crazy about Julius, and she was so much happier now that she had a puppy. Whenever something bad happened at school, all she had to do was think about him and she'd smile. Each afternoon, they shared a pack of cheese crackers. And her parents conceded that they'd been wrong about Helen; she took wonderful care of her puppy. Julius slept with Helen every night, lay on her feet as she did her homework, curled up next to her while she read, walked and played with her, and spent school days looking out the window, waiting for her to come home. When she neared the house, she could hear his howls.

Helen and Julius's connection changed her family. Her mother was still stunned by her daughter's sudden evolution into what she called a "puppy commando." As for her father, he seemed to look at Helen in a different way. He still wasn't thrilled about having a dog in the house, and Helen understood now that that probably wouldn't change. He really wasn't a dog person, but that was all right. She was, and he was okay with that.

Julius quickly became a master at getting people to scratch his soft pink belly. And, if they didn't, he would yowl. Helen said he was singing, and occasionally, they sang songs together. Her mother said it was the cutest thing she had ever seen, and her father loved to listen. During one of these impromptu concerts, the phone rang. Helen's mother answered it and then held the receiver out to her daughter. "It's for you," she whispered. "It's Iris, your friend from school."

Her parents exchanged a look. It was the first "friend" from school to call Helen.

Helen glanced up at her mother, utterly confused, then took the phone. "Hi, Iris," she said shyly.

"Hey, Helen," the girl replied, her voice stripped of its usual edge. "I heard you got a puppy. Can I come over sometime after school to meet him?"

"Sure," Helen said, a smile spreading across her face. "He'd like that."

Laura Passerby

LAURA JAMIESON DROVE THE SAME ROUTE TO HER JOB AS A RECEPtionist at a large suburban-Atlanta dental center for six years until the state decided to tear up the highway for a new overpass. This meant that for the next two years she would be getting off the main roads and driving through some rural landscape and farmland. The detour added almost forty-five minutes to her commute.

Some days she resented the construction, especially when it was raining or snowing. But some mornings, she didn't mind because she got to look at pretty farms and pastures instead of traffic and malls, and she felt the pleasant sensation of being reconnected to nature, not an easy thing to do in booming Atlanta.

It was some time during the third week of driving her new route that she noticed the decaying old yellow farmhouse and a black and gray dog chained to a tree out front.

Laura was almost past the farmhouse when she saw the dog. Something seemed wrong. In her neighborhood, dogs were sometimes out in yards but almost never tethered to trees.

The image of the dog tied to the tree stuck in her mind and bothered her all day as she answered phones, filled out insurance forms, and shuffled people in and out of the dentists' offices.

She had a dream about the dog that night. In the dream, the dog, maybe a German shepherd, was choking on the chain while hundreds of people drove by.

The next morning, Laura kept an eye out until she saw the farm looming up on the right after a new McMansion development. The farmhouse paint was peeling, and there were pieces of slate missing on the roof. The front and side yards were covered with junk—old tractors, plows, engines, trucks, and cars.

Laura pulled her Toyota Corolla slowly off to the side as she approached the farmhouse. It almost seemed abandoned, although when she looked off to her right, she saw an old red tractor far out in the field behind the house, black smoke belching from the exhaust pipe. She turned off the car engine and glanced off to the right. There was a giant old oak in front of the farmhouse, perhaps as old as the house itself, and tethered to it by the six- or seven-foot-long chain was the German shepherd, black and gray as she had remembered. He'd wrapped the chain partway around the tree and could only move a foot or two toward the road before being jerked back. She could see the water bowl well out of reach.

This dog was none of her business. But she got out of the

car and slowly approached him—she couldn't remember when she'd last even touched a dog—and he seemed overjoyed to see her, barking, wagging his tail, lunging, then getting jerked back again by the chain. She worried he would break his neck.

She put her hand out. If she got bit, she had only herself to blame.

The dog licked her hand. She felt as if he'd been waiting for her, desperate for her to help him. She knelt down on the grass and stroked his head. He was panting heavily, and spittle had caked up on his jaw and chest. There were scabs and scars all around the dog's neck from where he'd pulled against his collar. One was ugly, open, and raw.

She undid the hook that tethered the chain to the tree, then unraveled it from the trunk. She walked around the tree several times to do this, and the dog followed, almost eagerly. Then she refastened it. She leaned over to look at his threadbare collar. The tag said his name was Max. The rabies tag beneath was four years old.

"Max, come with me, come here," she said softly, and he enthusiastically obeyed.

When the chain was straight, she leaned over to pat him, and he licked her hand again and looked at her expectantly.

She thought about her father, a career military man who'd been killed in a bomb blast in Iraq six years earlier. Mind your own business, he always said. But if you see a wrong, try to right it.

The two seemed to be in conflict sometimes, but she knew what he meant. She needed to try to help this dog.

She walked back to the car and got out a piece of paper from her briefcase and a pen. She wrote a note:

Dear Sir, I found your dog wrapped around the tree. I helped him get the chain straight. In case you are not aware of this, he has wounds on his neck.

Laura, Passerby

She left the note in the mailbox.

Laura thought about Max all day and called her best friend, Nicki. "That's terrible," she said. "You ought to report him. That's abuse." Nicki was deeply into rescuing things—rabbits, birds, dogs, cats, anything. Nicki would rescue a hippo if she found one in the road.

Laura said she didn't want to get too involved. Maybe the farmer didn't know. Maybe he would read the note. Still, on her lunch hour, she shopped for dog biscuits and an antibiotic ointment Nicki recommended in case the situation did not improve.

She went online and looked up the regulations on tethering. It wasn't, she saw, illegal, unless the dog was choking or being deprived of food and water or on too small a lead. But this dog did indeed seem to be choking. She called the county hotline and left a message. No one called back.

When she drove home, it was dark and there was no sign of the dog.

The next morning, Max was not outside tied to the tree.

She didn't see him for two more days, and she thought that perhaps she'd done some good.

But at the end of the week he was there again, the chain taut around the tree, so he could barely move.

She got out of the car and approached him, and he was overjoyed to see her again. She looked around—and seeing no one—sat down next to the dog. She reached into her pocket for some biscuits and gave two or three to Max. He was happy to get them, scarfing them down.

"You're lonely, I bet," she said. "Nothing to do, tied to that tree all day."

Max seemed gentle, happy to let Laura touch him and get close. She saw that his claws were long, his coat was thick and heavily matted, and there were bits of leaves and feces stuck in the fur around his haunches. He smelled awful, and his teeth were stained a deep yellow.

She saw that his neck wounds were worse, and one looked especially angry, swollen, and infected. She took some ointment and rubbed it under the collar. He pulled back and put his mouth gently on her hand, as if to stop her, but she didn't stop, and he simply stared up at her, then gave up. She could hardly believe she had the nerve to do it.

She moved the water bowl closer. He drank eagerly.

That night, Laura went on to a rescue mailing list and posted a message about Max. The replies were fast and furious, and they all said the same thing.

"The dog is being abused," one woman from Charlotte wrote. "You have to get him out of there. It isn't stealing. It's stopping abuse before something terrible happens."

Laura had never stolen anything in her life.

No, she replied, she couldn't. It wasn't her dog.

"Then call the police," the woman said. "And if that doesn't work, give us the address and we'll find somebody to get him out, if you won't."

Laura logged off the site.

The third morning, she got bolder. She walked Max around the tree and left another note for the farmer.

I am concerned about your dog. Please take care of his wounds or I will contact the authorities.

Laura, Passerby

She peered around the back of the house and saw the tractor way off in the far corner of the pasture. Once again, she left the note in the mailbox.

When she got to the office that morning she called Animal Control again. There was no answer. So she called Nicki.

"Look," Nicki said, "you can't just leave Max out there. We've got to go get him. The rescue groups will take care of him. They have a sort of underground railway. They'll get him out of there and to a good home up north."

"You mean I should steal him?" Laura asked. "Because that's what I'd be doing."

"What are you going to do?" asked Nicki, "drive by there every morning and watch him choke to death a bit more each day?"

The next morning, Laura stopped by the farm. There was a longer chain than before, but Max had wrapped it around the tree again. He seemed happy to see her, jumping up and down so high she feared he'd choke himself. She dressed his neck wound, which looked better. He looked fed—wasn't skinny or emaciated. But she thought his eye was swollen, as if he'd been beaten. She took the farmer's name—Patterson—off the mailbox and wrote it down. She made sure Max was watered and fed and cleaned his wounds. He jumped up to lick her face.

It was hard for her to leave.

The next day she drove by the farm as usual, and forced herself not to look. When she came by on the way home, Max was not out in front.

She saw him the next three mornings and did not stop.

She refused to talk to Nicki about it anymore or answer the e-mails of the rescue group. Maybe it was time to leave Max alone. She'd done what she could do.

And yet she continued to dream about the dog every night.

A few days later, she called the number listed for Harold Patterson at the farm address and left a message. "Mr. Patterson, this is none of my business, I know, but I'm worried about your dog, Max, who's tethered to that tree every morning. He doesn't look well. Could you please call me about this?" And when she left her cell number, her voice and hands were shaking.

Friday, she pulled over to see if Max was okay, but he had wrapped himself so tightly around the tree that he appeared to be choking. His tongue was hanging down to the ground, and the collar had rubbed his wound raw again.

She unbuckled his collar and the dog jumped into her arms. Shaking, without even looking back, she led him to her car, opened the door, and Max lay down on the backseat.

She looked back toward the farm and thought she saw a curtain move in an upstairs window, but nobody appeared or tried to stop her.

As she started the engine, Max jumped into the shotgun seat, leaning over to lick her on the face. It was as if he'd been with her in the car a million times. He looked happy, at ease.

After calling her boss to take a personal day, Laura drove to a veterinary clinic near her home. She realized that she didn't even have a leash, so she carried Max into the office.

The receptionist looked at her dubiously. "Do you have an appointment?" The woman said this wasn't an emergency clinic, and they took animals only by appointment.

Laura had no idea what to do. She panicked, and then took Max back out to the car, putting him in on the passenger side before walking around to get in herself. Before she could get the key in the ignition, a young woman in a green surgical shirt came running out of the clinic. She looked no more than eighteen, Laura thought. She rolled down her window.

"I'm Marie, a vet tech here," she said. "He was tethered, wasn't he? You took him, didn't you? It's okay. I'm in animal rescue. He looks like he needs help."

Laura didn't really know what to say, so she simply nodded.

Marie stepped back and made a call on her cell. Then she returned to Laura's window, putting a hand on her shoulder.

"You did the right thing. Be at the Roundtree Mall in front of Home Depot tonight at nine P.M. You know where that is? Bring any of his things, if you have any. And dog food. And if you can, a contribution for travel and gas. These women don't have much money, and it's expensive to drive the long distances they drive."

Laura looked pleadingly at Marie. "I'm not a thief. I couldn't leave him there. He looked so pitiful. I saw him every day." Marie squeezed her hand. "It's okay. I know. We'll take care of it. You did a good thing. You don't need to tell me anything more."

And then she patted Max through the window and ran back into the clinic.

Laura didn't have any of Max's things, and she didn't have any dog food. She left the clinic lot—Max riding shotgun again—and drove to a nearby pet store, where she bought a twenty-five-pound bag of kibble, a new collar and leash, a clipper and brush, scissors, a dog bed, some balls, and a rawhide chew and put them in the back of the car.

LAURA SPENT THE DAY with Max. Walking him, talking to him, feeding him, dressing and bandaging his wounds. She brushed him carefully from head to tail, cutting out the burrs and clumps of twigs and grass embedded in his tail. He didn't like having his long nails clipped, but he submitted to it.

Laura found several tender bruises and many smaller cuts and scrapes and scabs around his body. His stool didn't look right to her. One of his eyes was running, and looked red.

And she was falling in love.

Max also seemed to be attaching himself to her, and reveling in the attention and care. She knew if she didn't get to the mall parking lot by nine, she'd never be able to let him go. She also knew Max wasn't safe with her, since he was stolen. If he were found with her, he might have to be returned.

At eight forty-five P.M., she pulled into an empty parking spot in front of the Home Depot and got out of the car with Max. She didn't know who she was looking for, so she stood in front of the car with the dog.

Just before nine P.M., a red minivan pulled alongside Laura's car, and a heavyset woman with curly brown hair stepped out and offered her hand. Laura heard barking from inside the van. The woman wore a blue sweatshirt with "Rescue: Be Good to Your Dog" stenciled on the back.

"I got this call this afternoon, and the timing was lucky. I was actually coming through from Florida up to New Jersey with a couple of pickups along the way. This is our boy?"

She leaned down and looked Max over, offering him her hand. She handed him a liver treat. She spent several minutes just talking to him and letting him get comfortable with her.

He looked at Laura curiously, but she could not bear to look him in the eyes.

The woman nodded. "I'll take him." Laura handed over Max's leash. The woman said, "Come on, boy," but he stopped and glanced back at Laura, who looked away.

Max disappeared around the other side of the van, and then the woman came back and collected his food and toys. Laura also gave her $100, which she accepted gratefully. "For gas and food," she said, then asked what would become of Max.

"He's already got two possible homes up in the Northeast. We'll check them out of course, although we know one—it's a farm, and they've taken dogs before and they're wonderful."

Before that, Max would spend a week at a volunteer veterinary clinic in Virginia, where he would have tests for worms and parasites. "If he's been tethered on a farm," she said, "he's a good bet for heartworm. He'll be evaluated to make sure there's no aggression or behavioral problems. Then onto his permanent home. If you want, we can e-mail you how he's doing."

Laura nodded. She felt sick, partly because Max was leaving and she would surely never see him again, and partly because of what she'd done.

The woman said good-bye, then turned and got into the van.

Over the next few weeks, Laura got a half dozen e-mails. There were no return e-mail addresses, only different names.

Max had made it to Virginia and been tested. He had severe heartworm, and the procedure to cure him was nearly fatal, but he came out of a coma and was fully recovered. He had kidney problems, and multiple contusions and bruises. The wounds on his neck were infected, and he had gum disease too.

One month after she left Max in the parking lot, she got a postcard from Rochester, New York. Max was on the front, standing in front of a barn, looking happy and proud, and behind him were at least a dozen sheep.

The postcard had a short message. "Max is great. He thanks you."

Laura knew without being told that this was the final message. She was delighted and relieved that Max was doing so well. But the burden of what she had done weighed heavily on her conscience. She still drove by the farm every day, and most days she couldn't bear to look at the tree. When she did, she saw the chain was still hanging off it, the water bowl upside down a few yards away.

One evening, she found herself pulling into the farmhouse driveway. She turned off the ignition, took a deep breath, and then walked up to the front door and slammed the knocker three times.

After a few minutes, she heard a noise inside the house, and then the door opened. Silhouetted in the hallway light was a thin, tall, ruddy-faced man who looked to be in his early sixties. He was wearing boots, jeans, and an old work shirt that was stained with what appeared to be sweat and grease marks. He had one- or two-day-old stubble on his chin. His face was sad, tired. But the shock of white hair hanging over his forehead made him look both handsome and dignified, like an old western sheriff in a TV movie.

"Mr. Patterson. My name is Laura."

The old man nodded. "Laura Passerby."

She was startled.

"That's what you said in your note."

Now that she was standing there in front of him, she wasn't sure what she had come to say.

"You stole my dog, didn't you," the farmer said rather than asked.

A chill wind whipped her jacket and blew her hair across her face. He looked at her closely, and then beckoned for her to step into the hallway, out of the wind.

"Yes, I did. I took him, sir," she said, as she stepped inside. "He's up in the Northeast, on a farm with sheep. He's loved and happy."

The farmer's eyes blazed. "He'll do well then. He knows how to work sheep," the old man said. "He worked sheep here until last year."

"Well, he was suffering. He had heartworm, and his neck was infected."

The farmer just looked her. "I brought him in for a couple of days after I got your notes. He jumped out of the second-story window, and then through the screen on the kitchen window and banged himself up. You couldn't ever leave him anywhere that he couldn't get out of. Except that tree."

Harold Patterson crossed his arms. "Listen, Laura Passerby. Max was my dog. He is a good boy. And I cared for him a good deal. The farm is up for sale. My wife passed two years ago. My boys won't work on the farm, and I can't make it work anymore. Tried long enough. The milk prices are so low I had to let the dairy cows go, and then I sold off the sheep to pay the taxes—you see all the development around here. I'm the last to go. I've been cleaning up the fields so I can sell them, and I'm going to need all the money from the farm to pay off my loans and debts. I'm moving to South Carolina where my two boys live. Max was coming with me."

This was not what she'd expected.

"I'll own up to neglecting him a bit lately," he said. "I've got some health issues myself now, and Max is clever and kept getting out of the house and running into the road. Was going to get himself killed. He kept chewing through the collars so I put out a chain to hold him. My grandfather tethered his dog, and so did my father. Just so he could be outside and not cooped up in the house, or running under the tractor wheels. I knew about the neck. I couldn't do the vet bills right now—I can't do the mortgage either. But I would have found a way to take care of him."

"I'm sorry," she said. "I thought I was saving the dog. I still think so."

The farmer stepped outside and motioned for her to follow. "Maybe you did save the dog. It probably was a good decision, Laura Passerby. It probably was. I appreciate your coming here. I was worried about Max. I called the police and told them the dog was missing. A neighbor got your license one morning when you were snooping around here. But I didn't give it to them. I figured he probably went to a good place."

She nodded.

"Max was well fed and loved and he slept on the foot of my bed every night of his life. He had shelter from the rain and cold, and until a year or so ago he had a lot of good work to do and he did it. Maybe you think I'm an evil man for tying him up to that tree, and maybe I am. But maybe it's just a way of life you don't understand, and you have no right to judge it or to take my dog from me."

Laura could see how embarrassed the farmer was over his inability to take care of his dog. Everyone she knew told her that she'd done the right thing. And maybe she had. But looking into this man's eyes, it was hard to know for sure.

The farmer looked up at the sky, and then turned to her. The wind blew through the farm and the old house groaned and creaked.

"I'm glad he's in a better place," he said. "I am glad of that." Then he started to turn back to the house. "I'll say good-bye now. It took courage for you to come here, young lady. But don't steal things anymore, okay?"

"Yes, sir," she said.

The Dog Who Kept Men Away

STACY SIPPED FROM HER DUNKIN' DONUTS COFFEE CUP AND LOOKED over at the mediator for some guidance. He was sipping his own coffee and sorting through some papers.

More than anything, she wanted to get out of there. She hated this room, a spare, empty conference room with bare white walls and two small windows looking out over an enormous mall parking lot. There was an anemic pale cactus in the middle of the table. Why would you have a cactus in a conference room in Sandusky, Ohio?

There were two photographs on the walls, a stock shot of some horses in a field from the Saratoga racetrack in upstate New York (about as relevant to Sandusky as cactus), and a shot of one of the roller coasters from the nearby Cedar Point Amusement Park, where Stacy had worked part-time the summer she was sixteen, and where she had met Jamie, the bored, sad-looking young man sitting across from her, staring out the window.

The first two mediation sessions had been awful—tears, yelling, fury. Then, in the third, things settled down and they finally reached an agreement. Until Jamie broke it.

The end of her twelve-year marriage deserved a better room, she thought. Or maybe not. Maybe it was just right.

Jamie, her soon-to-be ex, was yawning. He seemed distracted, eager to go home. He told the lawyer that his hours had been cut back at the Lobster Den and he was looking to sell his truck and find a cheaper apartment. Maybe even move the hell out of Ohio and go south where there might be some work. In the meantime, he had no money for Stacy.

Jamie was allergic to jobs. And he would never move, Stacy knew, especially as long as his mother was alive and getting her pension from GM.

The mediator collected his papers and handed them to her. He told her again that she didn't have to forgive the nine grand, that a judge would make him pay her the money. She didn't care. She just wanted to be free of him. She signed the papers.

Stacy looked at her watch. She had just thirty minutes to get back to the nursing home and her job as a physical-therapy aide, helping the disabled elderly recover from and deal with strokes, accidents, surgeries, their own failing bodies. She loved the job, loved the feeling of really helping people, even if the ending was always the same. It was a lot of loss and suffering for $9 an hour, the same money her friend Sandra made working the fries boiler at McDonald's. People in America obviously care a lot more about their fast food than their sick old people.

Back in her car, alone, she felt a flash of rage at Jamie. He'd been to Florida twice with his new girlfriend, gotten that new truck, a big flat-screen TV. And here she was living month to month, close to maxing out her credit card, looking for a part-time weekend job. He didn't give a shit. She saw now that he never had.

Maybe she would never have another relationship. Maybe she was destined to not have a family, never be a mother. Jamie wasn't the only jerk she had encountered. Since they'd separated, there had been a whole string of them. One dumped her, and she dumped two. The one she liked had turned out to be gay. Sitting in the car, she resolved that she was over men, and a profound sense of loneliness swept over her.

STACY LATER SAID an invisible hand had taken control of her.

She found herself driving south on Route 9. Her job was in the opposite direction. So was her apartment. There was nothing in this direction but the new county prison and the Northern Ohio Animal Rescue League.

Stacy speed-dialed her boss and left a message saying she was tied up at the doctor's office and would be a half hour late.

She walked into the main lobby of the shelter and signed in at the visitors' desk. It was not the first time she'd been there. Several years earlier, she'd come by to get a puppy to surprise Jamie, but he wasn't interested in taking care of a dog, he said, and claimed he was allergic to animals with fur. She didn't believe him, but she didn't think it was fair to the puppy to keep him, so she returned the dog. One other time, she'd come by just to look at the dogs and cats up for adoption, but she hadn't even tried to bring one home.

"I'm here to look at the dogs up for adoption," she said, once inside the lobby, and the woman smiled and handed her a form to fill out. The county wasn't as touchy or demanding as some of the private rescue groups. They had a lot of dogs coming through there, and they had to put a lot of them down. There weren't any home inspections.

Stacy was ushered into the back by a staffer named Judith and a volunteer named Marge and shown into the "Get Acquainted room" where people and dogs got to meet and check each other out. There were seven new dogs in the kennel. Two seemed to be lost pets—a black Lab and a poodle—and there would be a thirty-day hold on them in case their owners came looking for them, which was often the case with purebred, well-cared-for dogs. Another, a sad-eyed Boston terrier, was found in an apartment with his owner who had been dead for several days.

A Rottweiler and a mixed-breed were still in quarantine until their health and temperament could be evaluated. The sixth was a terrier who had been injured—hit by a car or motorcyle, they thought, and brought in by the police. They weren't sure he would make it.

"And the seventh?" Stacy asked. Judith and Marge looked at each other.

"That's Dolly." Marge paused. "She's a big dog. A Rottweiler-pit mix, we think."

Stacy waited.

Judith looked at her paperwork. "She's a powerful dog and somewhat intimidating."

Stacy smiled. "That's a good start," she said. "What's the downside?"

Judith smiled. "Nothing that we've seen. She's housebroken, easy with people, a real sweetie."

"Is she really housebroken?"

"Yes," said Marge, looking through her notes. "She's

well-trained, knows basic obedience commands, and is very healthy and strong." She added: "We don't want her to just go anyplace. Whoever adopts her has to understand the situation."

"Situation?"

Marge explained that Dolly was first seen around the campus of Sandusky Community College, which was set on a one-hundred-acre estate on the edge of the town. She had clearly been abandoned, and was living outside, foraging through garbage and eating food that some of the students would leave for her on the edge of the parking lot.

Dolly became a sort of mythical figure to the students at the college. One student, a volunteer at the shelter, was able to lure Dolly into a crate with a steak. She must have been very hungry because she went for it.

A few minutes later, the three women went down the hallway and came to a heavy metal door plastered with warnings about entering, which Marge pushed open.

Dolly was indeed a big dog, with a Rottweiler body and a pit-bull face. She had a wide, square face and broad, muscular shoulders. She was pretty fierce to look at.

But Stacy thought she was gorgeous. She was the color of snow and had the most beautiful round blue eyes that Stacy had ever seen on an animal.

"Pits are hard to place," Marge said. "If Dolly doesn't get a home, she'll probably end up getting put down."

But for some reason, Stacy couldn't do it. She thanked Judith and Marge. They said they understood; it was no good getting a dog if you didn't want one. It wasn't doing the dog any favor.

Stacy walked outside, and drove to work. On the way, she thought, Screw Jamie. She was counting on that money to pay her credit card off and fix her car. Why did he always, always have to let her down?

That night she had a dream. Dolly was in the shelter for days and days. A vet came in and pronounced her unfit for adoption. He took her into the procedure room to give her an injection that would kill her. Then the dog spoke: *Why didn't you save me?*

Stacy sat up in bed, sweating.

In the morning, she drove to the shelter, sitting in the parking lot for fifteen minutes before she saw Marge pull in. She looked up as Stacy got out of her car.

"Good morning," Marge said, smiling.

An hour later, Stacy and Dolly pulled out of the shelter parking lot and headed home. Dolly sat quietly in the passenger seat, watching the buildings and cars slide by. Once in a while, she would turn to Stacy and eye her curiously.

Stacy saw in Dolly's face a reflection of her own need.

Back at the apartment, Dolly was a pussycat. She preferred the floor to sofas. She ate almost anything. She would sit at Stacy's feet like some Egyptian statue, off in her own world, silent, almost regal.

The first time Stacy walked Dolly in the park, the dog bristled when a man came walking by. She let a couple of teenage girls pet her, but then she lunged after a jogger as he sped past. Some people—especially those with children—stayed back when they saw Dolly coming. She could definitely clear a sidewalk.

One afternoon, Jamie came by—as usual, unannounced and uninvited—to ask if he could pick up the CDs he'd left in a box in the basement storage area. Dolly came right through the screen door at him and chased him down the walk. She attached herself to his foot as he jumped through the open window of his truck, and she came back with his Nike, offering it to Stacy with a wag of her tail. Then she ran back to the truck, scratching at the door and leaving slobber marks on the window as Jamie screamed inside.

He called her on her cell. "Stacy, what's wrong with you? You ought to get rid of that crazy dog before you get sued. It ate my fucking shoe!"

Well, she said, she was sorry. She'd just deduct the cost of the sneaker from the $9,000 he should have paid her. Best to call ahead next time.

A month later, Dolly had fully settled in, and the two ladies had a routine set. Stacy was feeling some of her confidence return and decided it was time get back out there on the dating scene.

Her first date was with Carlos, an orderly from work who came by to take her to a staff party at the nursing home. Dolly kept him pinned in a corner by the door while Stacy got ready. When she came downstairs, he looked ashen. She was pleased to note that Dolly didn't actually bite or attack him. Later, Carlos declined to accept her halfhearted invitation to come in for coffee.

On the second date, Dolly simply growled at Jerry who did accept a halfhearted invitation for coffee, and foolishly invited himself over to the couch and put his arm around Stacy's shoulder. Dolly then invited *herself* over and took his shoe in her mouth, fixing him with a deadly stare and growling. Jerry moved to another seat across the room, and left soon after, Dolly's growls following him all the way.

Okay, so Dolly didn't like men. At first, this was upsetting. But then Stacy decided she couldn't really blame her. She wasn't all that crazy about them either.

One morning, Stacy's supervisor, Sally, was walking down the hall with a handsome young man Stacy had never seen before. Sally stopped and introduced her to Mark, who was a social worker, the facility's new ombudsman. Stacy felt a vaguely familiar flutter in her chest.

Later that day in the cafeteria, Mark asked if he could join her for lunch. He didn't talk much about himself, which was a new experience for Stacy. Trying to make small talk, she asked him if he was a Cubs or Indians fan, which was usually a conversation-starter with the men she had known, and he said he wasn't into sports that much. But he loved dogs.

Stacy told him about Dolly, and he seemed fascinated. When Stacy told him how Dolly had eaten Jamie's sneaker, he said the dog was a "keeper," for sure.

The next day, Mark was back again for lunch. And the next day also. Stacy was off that weekend, but first thing Saturday morning, Mark called her at home. Would she like to take a walk along the lake? It was a beautiful morning.

Two hours later, Mark, Stacy, and Dolly were walking along the water near Cedar Point Amusement Park. The giant roller coasters hovered over them. Mark had insisted that she bring Dolly. Stacy had been wary, and Dolly was clearly not impressed. She fixed him with a deathly stare and growled when Mark even looked at her.

But Stacy noted that he handled the dog's response differently from the other men. He simply ignored Dolly. On the walk, if he came too close to Stacy, Dolly would move in and show her teeth. After a few minutes, Stacy saw Mark reach into his pocket and toss something on the ground. Dolly veered ahead and scarfed it up.

"Do you always keep meat in your pocket?" she asked him, laughing.

"I like to make a good impression," he said with a smile.

At the end of the path, they sat down and talked. Mark told her about school and his decision to go into health care and social work rather than law. He wanted to do something meaningful with his life, not just make money. He asked her about her marriage, her work, her life. He seemed to listen, a different and unsettling experience for Stacy. She didn't quite believe it was for real.

Mark was gentle and quiet, and that took some getting used to. She thought she detected a stubborn streak, but she wasn't sure. She reminded herself to be cautious. First impressions were just first impressions, but the truth was she liked being around him.

Dolly, however, remained vigilant, growling every now and then, though not as intensely.

Every once in a while, Mark would reach into his pocket and toss some beef jerky down onto the ground. Dolly would scarf it up. He never looked at Dolly or spoke to her.

After a while, Stacy saw that Dolly was paying a lot of attention to Mark, especially to his hands and pockets.

They stopped for coffee at a local diner, and when they came back out, Dolly growled and lunged toward Mark, who started and backed off. Stacy held her leash tightly and told her to be quiet. God, she thought, I finally meet a nice guy and I have a dog that will chew him up or keep him away.

She told Mark she had enjoyed the walk.

He called the next morning and asked if he could stop by on his way to work. She was puzzled—it was early—but she said yes. A few minutes later, the doorbell rang. Dolly barked and rushed to the door. When she opened it, Mark stood there with a Ziploc bag filled with a dozen hot-dog bits—cooked and pungent. Dolly growled and huffed but was intrigued by the bag. Mark tossed her a piece of hot dog, and she caught it on the fly, then looked for another. She got one more, than another, until all the bits were gone. And then Mark left.

He hadn't talked to Stacy that much. It was almost as if he was coming just to see Dolly. It was a little weird. But the next morning, Stacy let him come over again before heading to work. Once again, he threw bits of hot dog to Dolly. He never spoke to her or looked her in the eye. The following Sunday, he came by and sat on the porch with Dolly and Stacy. While they talked, Mark tossed beef jerky to the dog.

Over the following weeks, Mark and Stacy went to the movies a couple of times, and then out to dinner. One evening at Stacy's place, he reached over to pet Dolly, but she growled and he pulled his hand back.

Every time he came to the apartment, he brought treats for Dolly. Stacy was amazed by how consistent he was. She was also a bit perplexed. He still seemed more interested in Dolly than in her. He never tried to sit on the couch with Stacy, never tried to touch or kiss her.

She told Mark she was getting a little confused about this strange trio. Was he dating her? Or Dolly? Or both?

"I just enjoy dogs," he said. "But I don't want to be making any trouble. I don't want to upset you."

After that, he disappeared for several weeks. He avoided her at the nursing home and didn't call. She missed him. And she thought Dolly missed him too. She seemed to be watching for him in the mornings.

Then one day, without explanation, he called up and asked if he could come by.

She said yes.

The three slipped quietly back into their old routine. It was, Stacy had to admit, a lovely friendship.

Mark started bring her small things when he visited. Romance novels. Judy Collins CDs. Asian pears. Chocolate. She wondered how he knew what she liked, and then she remembered. He had asked. They were always little things, inexpensive things. Nothing too showy, nothing that made her too uncomfortable. She told him not to bother, that he didn't need to give her things, but he always smiled, and said that if he had to, he wouldn't have.

She realized Jamie wouldn't have known to get her any of those things, not even after twelve years.

Dolly continued to challenge and intimidate men. As for Mark, she kept an eye on him, kept her distance, but she had softened. She growled and grumped when he came in, but she also was eager for the rain of treats and didn't seem to see his arrival as a dangerous intrusion.

After several months of beef-jerky and hot-dog visits, Mark showed up with a barbecued steak. He asked Stacy if he could borrow a knife, and he chopped it up into chunks, put it back in the plastic bag he'd brought it in, and went out onto the porch.

Dolly did not growl at him. She followed him out and sat next to him, as alert and focused as a Westminster show dog.

Mark just walked around with the steak in a plastic bag. Dolly got more and more focused on him. He tossed a couple of pieces. By now, it had become a kind of game, this tossing and catching of food, and Dolly liked it. She *loved* it.

On the previous visit, she had lain down in front of Mark

and gone to sleep, the first time Stacy had ever seen her do that. And since he never touched Stacy or came near her or tried to sit next to her on the couch, Dolly's protective instincts began to soften. No threat.

This day, on the porch, Mark looked Dolly in the eye. "Sit," he said, firmly but clearly. Dolly sat. "Lie down," he said. She lay down.

He leaned forward—he had a piece of steak in his hand—and patted her head. She wagged her tail.

He told her to "come," and to "lie down" again. She did.

He gave her two more chunks of steak. Then he asked Stacy if he could take Dolly for a walk alone, and she hesitated for a second—it seemed to hit her that there was more going on than a walk—but she said yes. The two were gone for an hour.

When they came back, Mark said they had gone to the park. Dolly had chased balls and played tug-of-war with a rubber toy he had bought. Dolly, sated and exhausted, came into the house and crawled into her dog bed and collapsed. Soon, her snoring filled the room. She paid no attention to where Mark was or wasn't.

Stacy's eyes teared suddenly. Dolly looked very tired, but also very happy. She had never thought to do those things with her, even though she loved her very much. It made her happy to see it. She thought Mark was so sweet to do it. He had to have a big heart. You couldn't fool a dog. She remembered how Dolly had run Jamie right out of her driveway and her life.

Dolly's snores deepened. Stacy was on her own. The dog who kept men away was not.

Mark asked if he could come over to the couch and sit with her, and Stacy said yes.

Barn Cat

She heard the crickets start up—the signal for her to begin work—and she crawled out from behind the coop, sashayed past the rooster, who was watching her, and then headed out into the night. She soaked up the late-summer smells and sounds of the forest, moving freely back and forth from the woods and meadows, then into the cavernous barn with its machines, animals, and towers of stacked hay.

Evening was her favorite hunting and stalking time. The birds were still awake and making noise. There was little light, and breezes carried the scents of the land. She moved through the pastures and woods like a shadow, slowly and carefully, creeping through the tall grass, through the bushes and reeds.

She was in her element—watching, listening, waiting, stalking, catching things. Sometimes she ate them and sometimes she played with them, tortured them, or even let them go. There were mice everywhere, but every now and then she came across something different—a snake, a baby rabbit, a wounded bird. Wherever she went, she left a trail of dead and dismembered creatures, methodically pursued, joyfully killed.

The cat always knew just where she was and what was around her. She stayed away from roads and clear paths. She was not heard or seen. Few of the animals out in the meadow or the woods could see the way she could, or be as still for so long. Her patience and focus were extraordinary. She could feel movement even before she heard or saw it. She sat, her body stiff, eyes widened, ears straight up and pointed forward. She waited.

Unlike most other animals, she spent her life alone but did not understand the concept of loneliness.

SHE CIRCLED BACK near the barn and listened to the rats moving around in the stone wall. She seemed to sense that killing the rats was her purpose, her mission, and she pursued them coldly and with ruthless efficiency. She knew there were not many left.

Her eyes were fixed on the crevices between the rocks for any sign of movement. She was still for a long time, and then she heard a pebble drop to the ground. The nose of a large rat appeared, its mate hovering behind it. She heard the tiny squeals of their babies back in the nest, hungry for the food that the mother and father rats were heading out to find.

The first rat hit the ground, then skittered off to the rear of the barn, where the cows were and the smells were strong and rich. She waited until he'd reached the grain pans. He would gorge on the grain, stuffing his cheeks with enough to bring back.

She waited, even more still than before, her eyes never leaving the cleft in the wall. Soon another rat appeared, the mother, looking anxiously back and forth. When the mother rat landed on the ground, the cat leapt from her hiding place in the grass, landing right on her back. She knew the rat would fight to protect her babies, sensed it, and, long sharp claws out, she grabbed the shocked, stunned mother on both sides of her neck. The rat fought back savagely, crying out and biting her attacker on the shoulder, drawing blood. The two of them rolled around, one screaming a warning, the other silent and relentless. Inside the house, the useless dog heard something and barked. A human voice said, "Jake, ssssh." When it was over, the cat hopped up onto the stone wall and licked her own blood from her throbbing shoulder. Then she was still again.

The male rat had heard the struggle and came scurrying quickly around the corner where the cat was waiting for him. She pounced so that he didn't have time to struggle, nor did he have a mother's instincts to power him. She had shocked him and she used this advantage. When she was done, she dragged both bodies into the rear of the barn where she would finish with them later. Then she sat and waited for the babies. She could hear them squeaking in hunger. It wouldn't be long.

At the end of her evening hunts, as the sun rose and filled the barn with its yellow glow, the cat would slide under the fence, hop up to the broken window, crawl in, and land next to the big rooster who clucked and grumbled as he guarded his hens. She would jump over the chicken wire and sit underneath one of the overhanging roosts, where it was warm and comfortable. There was hay and straw, and it was out of sight.

The rooster had not liked her presence at first. When she invaded the roosts, he puffed up his chest, spread his wings, moved in front of the hens, and clucked imperiously. She paid him no mind. He was a tough rooster, and had pecked at the farmer and his wife when they came too close to his hens. But he eventually grew comfortable with the barn cat, and now when she approached, he would still squawk, but without menace.

She ignored the rooster's bluster. She felt at ease with him.

This old, fading rooster and this ferociously independent cat had reached an understanding. He sensed that she meant no harm to him or his charges. The connection between them was part of the mystery of animals, which humans could not fathom and the animals themselves did not consider.

She did not bond with the other creatures on the farm. Sometimes when she hunted behind the farmhouse, the big brown dog the farmer called Jake would sense or smell her and come to the window or the porch. She had only to meet his eyes and he would whine, growl a bit, then move back into the house. She was unfathomable to him as well, a quiet creature who seemed to need nothing, and would kill almost anything. Jake was now used to finding bits of frogs, bird's heads, dead snakes, and the carcasses of rats, moles, chipmunks, and mice all over the farm. They all had her smell on them.

SHE WAS NOT COMFORTABLE with any humans. She avoided people, especially when she sensed they were watching her. She did not trust or comprehend them. But sometimes she was drawn to the farmer's wife, who appeared in the barn in bitter cold or storms and left hot milk or soup with meat in it for her. The woman would call out to her—"Hey, cat! Hey, cat!"—in a soft and pleasing voice, and the cat would sometimes show herself, but always from a distance. When the woman saw her, she would nod and smile. She knew better than to pressure a barn cat. "Something to warm you up, give you strength," she would say before leaving.

The cat would never appear for the farmer though. When she heard him come out of the farmhouse and walk toward the barn, she would melt away, disappearing up into the tall reaches of the hayloft where she hunted bats and rats and mice and slept, or she would head out into the woods.

ON THE DAY the barn cat joined the farm, a Chevy pickup trailing a cloud of dust had pulled up to the big red barn on Callaway Road in Belcher, New York. An old farmer uncoiled himself from the truck and moved a few steps toward the barn with the signature stiff and slow walk of all veteran dairy farmers whose knees are shot from years of milking twice a day. A big German shepherd came bounding out from behind the barn, barking until he recognized the old man, and then rushed over to sniff the box and growl.

"Hey, Jake, old boy," said the man, setting the box down on the ground. "I brought you a barn cat to get rid of those rats Pete is having so much trouble with," he continued, rubbing the big dog's ears. "I had a litter of six of 'em, and I got rid of five and kept this one for Pete."

Barn cats were always having unwanted litters, and farmers often "got rid of them." Some men shot the superfluous creatures, or else drowned or poisoned them. Nobody talked much about the unsavory business, but everybody knew about it.

From the farmers' point of view, there wasn't much choice. Even the shelters didn't want them, had no room for them. Barn cats were almost never spayed or neutered, nor taken to vets, and if you let them breed unchecked, the barns would soon be overrun with cats and waste, sometimes disease.

A persistent meow came from the box. Jake whined and circled, his ears back. A man in a red Agri-Mark cap came out of the barn, waved, and called Jake back.

"Hey, Pete," called the farmer with the box.

"Hey, Darryl," said Pete. "Thanks for bringing the cat over. These rats are getting big as rabbits. One of them bit Jake here, and I had to take him to the vet for rabies shots."

Darryl looked over at Jake, who had an adhesive bandage taped around his rear left leg. The dog nosed the box and growled.

"That's our new rat killer," Pete told Jake. "Leave her alone if you know what's good for you." Jake didn't always know what was good for him, but he was obedient, so he stepped away from the box.

"I think she'll do right by you," Darryl said. "I don't see much of her—I had to trap her with a piece of fish and she nearly bit my arm off—but I think she's a real hunter."

Pete thanked Darryl, who waved and clambered back into his truck. He picked up the box and brought it into the barn, followed closely by Jake.

A huge red rooster rounded the corner and let out an

ear-splitting crow. "Jeez, Argyle, shut up," said the farmer. A score of Orpington hens trailed the rooster industriously, pecking at waste and bugs.

Pete put the box on top of one of the hay bales stacked in the rear of the barn. He opened it, stepped back, and waited a few seconds, but nothing happened. The cows were lowing anxiously from the milking area. "I got to get back in there," he told the dog, and headed to his charges.

Jake sat on his haunches and waited. He knew there was a cat in there; he could smell her. But there was no movement. He edged closer and reached his nose toward the open end of the box. He heard the hiss and felt the claws long before he saw the cat's luminous green eyes.

Jake yelped and ran down the aisles of the barn, past the hay bales, and into the milking bay where Pete was kneeling down, attaching a suction hose to a cow's teat. Jake had spent his whole life around cows, and he'd been kicked once or twice. Cows rarely looked for trouble unless they were provoked, and the dog had learned to leave them alone. He now knew to leave the cat alone too.

Pete looked down at the bloody marks on the dog's snout and shook his head and smiled. He got up, called Jake over to the side of the barn, and put some antibiotic powder on his scratches.

"Well, this one may work out," he told the dog, scratching Jake's ears for comfort.

PETE DID NOT NAME his barn cats, or get close to them. He didn't bring them into the farmhouse or feed them unless it was well below zero for days, and even then, he would only let his wife put out some leftover soup or cheap kibble from the convenience store. He made a point of not getting too attached to animals, especially barn cats, who had short and difficult lives.

Some farmers put heat lamps out for their cats in the winter, but there had been several awful barn fires as a result, and so Pete's cats fended for themselves. The cat was not high on his list of worries, but sometimes he looked around the barn, wondering where she might go to stay warm at night.

He cautioned his wife about feeding her too often: "She'll get spoiled and wait to be fed rather than hunting the rats and mice." He wanted the cat to be hungry. Otherwise she'd just be another animal to feed, and he needed her to work. Pete had had increasingly serious problems with aggressive rats ever since he'd turned the tractor over while hauling some silage into the concrete bunkers where it was stored for the winter. Silage, a fermented corn mix used to feed the cows in cold weather, drew rats as well as raccoons and birds.

Pete had seen the cat for the first time a week after she had arrived and had her initial dustup with Jake. The dog had whined and growled, looking out at the big pasture behind the barn. There the farmer could see the cat creeping quietly toward the field. Smart girl—it was good hunting ground. He held up his field glasses and saw that she was a beauty, with glossy brown and black fur and striking, almost eerie eyes. She carried herself with great presence. She was not skinny and moth-eaten like most of the barn cats he'd had. She was different.

He had not seen her since.

Though she never showed herself to the farmer, she knew where he was at all times. She often watched him as he moved about the farm and did his chores. Sometimes she peered out from the vast stacks of hay bales, sometimes from a branch high up in one of the farm's apple or maple trees. Often she slithered through the tall grass in the meadow to keep an eye on him.

Many days, he saw traces of her. He knew she was at work. He noticed the first dead rat within days of her arrival—a huge thing lying by the entrance to the barn, almost like a calling card. He found two more the next day, and a dozen over the following week. Various parts of birds, mice, snakes, and moles—also her handiwork—littered the farm. He marveled at how effective a killing machine she was. The rats were becoming scarce.

She was doing her job, and one day, like all of the other barn cats he had ever known, she would disappear. Shot by a hunter or a kid with a .22. Hit by a car or truck. Swept up by an owl or picked off by a clever coyote or fox. Caught by a stray dog. Poisoned. Weakened by hunger, stricken with worms, parasites, rabies, or one of the many other diseases that afflicted barn cats. They never got old. They tended not to last long.

THE FIRST FEW DAYS after she crawled out of that cardboard box, the cat hid up in the hay bales. She caught a few mice, swatted some bats out of the air, and ate moths and spiders. When she got thirsty, she crept down to the barn floor and sipped from the cows' water trough.

Cautiously, she explored the vast barn, which sat next to an old white farmhouse, bookended by pastures on one side and woods on the other. She smelled the cats that had been there before her and the two others still in the barn. One was old and rheumy, waiting to die, the other a frail female with an injured leg.

The female challenged her but the fight was quick. After that, neither of the other cats wanted any trouble. She staked out her territory right away: the big barn where the hay was stored and the fields and woods beyond the farmhouse. The other cats could have the smaller pole barn and the pasture behind it. They stayed out of her way.

She slept in the mornings and again in the afternoons when the sun was high and strong and warm. At dusk, she listened to the rats and the mice skittering around for food and burrowing into their crevices and nests. The mice were easy pickings, but the rats were big and could fight back. She had to be still, come at them from above or behind, startle and stun them, kill them quickly. Then she'd find their nests and kill their babies.

Later in the evenings, when the rats were in their burrows, there were other creatures to hunt. Bats, of course, and the mice, but also squirrels, baby rabbits, and moles in the meadow. She was always near a tree, or had an eye on one, in case a coyote or fox came out of the woods to hunt for rabbits. She knew every crevice and every low branch in every tree all through the woods around the barn. One night, betrayed by a full moon, she was nearly caught by two coyotes, but she was able to scramble up a tree. She stayed in the high branches all night, and the next morning she caught a songbird as it hopped out of its nest and began to sing.

Two nights later, a gray fox chased after her. She made a frantic run back across the meadow and into the barn and found herself face-to-face with the rooster, who was awake and patrolling. She rubbed against him, and he flapped his wings but didn't move away.

HIGH UP in the barn, the cat loved to leap up, grab a barn swallow, and then hop from bale to bale with the bird in her teeth. She did it gleefully, and if the farmer or his wife had ever seen her, they would have sworn she was dancing. She was mesmerized by the giant spiderwebs and she clawed at them, fascinated, catching the frantic spiders, eating them or watching them scurry away.

Some nights she crept up onto the farmhouse porch, where she lay on one of the farmer's hammocks, listening to the noises from inside the house. She loved to look in the window and see the flickering images on the box in the corner, hear the farmer and his wife talking or the phones ringing, smell the food cooking on the stove. Once in a while she thought the farmer's wife saw her, and when she sensed she was being watched, she would vanish, fleeing into the woods or back to the barn. But she liked being close to the bustle of the farmhouse.

She was not like the dog though, of whom she was contemptuous. She did not bow and scrape for food, or follow humans around. She did not play with them, or want to be scratched or touched by them. She did not want to be inside the house, trapped and helpless. She could take care of herself, find something to eat, seek out a warm spot by the cows, or the generators, or bask in the rays of the sun.

The farm was full of places she loved, but when her work was done and the night was quiet, she felt most comfortable in the barn near the rooster. She was the only creature on the farm who didn't take the rooster seriously, although his crow, coming at odd times these days, would sometimes startle her and ruin her secret naps under the roost. At some point every day she found herself checking in with the rooster, who had gotten used to her, accepted her, even watched out for her.

When she came into the barn, the two of them would settle down, one next to the other. She would nap there, or just sit and look out the windows toward the farmhouse. Once in a while, she rubbed against the rooster, and although he was startled at first, he didn't get flustered or huffy, didn't crow or flap his wings at her. He seemed to like her company, and she his. This was not something she thought about; it was just something that happened.

IN THE AUTUMN, almost all of the rats were gone. One by one, she had hunted them down, slaughtered the adults, killed the babies. There were still some mice in the barn, but there would always be some, just as there would always be some bats.

That November, as winter approached and the days turned gray and the nights cold, the farmer came into the barn and saw the rooster lying on his side by the chicken roost inside the pen where the chickens slept. He knew the old Rhode Island Red was tiring, and was not surprised to see him near death.

But he *was* surprised to see the tortoiseshell cat—the one who had cleared the barn of rats—lying next to him. She sat up and looked him in the eye, but she didn't run. The farmer was taken aback. The cat, who had never allowed him to get close, was sitting coolly just a few yards in front of him, her green eyes meeting his.

He reached into his pocket for his cell phone and called his wife, who appeared shortly with a saucer of warm milk. The two of them took in the strange sight of the cat sitting next to the rooster. "She's protecting him from the other chickens," the farmer's wife said. Chickens were ruthless when one of their flock was dying. They would often peck the dying chicken to death, starting with the eyes. "She's watching over him. Keeping him company."

The rooster was lying down, able to lift his head and attempt some feeble crows, but otherwise almost inert.

"He's dying," the farmer told his wife. "I'll go get the ax. I'm not wasting a bullet on a chicken."

"Pete, just hold up," she said quietly but with authority. "She's sitting with him. Let's leave them alone."

"Why do you think she's protecting Argyle?"

"I don't know," she said, shrugging, "But she's clearly not leaving him."

The farmer's wife had witnessed a few of these peaceable-kingdom friendships—a horse and a sheep, a donkey and a lamb, a dog and a hen. There was no understanding these odd pairs, she thought—they could be explained only by the Lord. But that animals could reach so far down into themselves to find loyalty and friendship always touched her deeply.

The farmer and his wife left the barn.

For the next three days and nights, the cat sat with the old rooster. If she left to hunt or eliminate, neither the farmer nor his wife saw her go. In the daylight, the cat hung back a few paces, but at night, she curled up next to the old bird, leaning against him. If any of the hens came near, the cat would get up and hiss, and they would retreat hastily. Although the farmer's wife never saw the cat eat, the saucer was always empty when she came to replace it. Sometimes she sat down in a corner of the roost and held out her hand to the cat. Sometimes, when her husband wasn't around, she spoon-fed the rooster.

On the second day of her vigil, the cat approached the farmer's wife, sniffed her hand, and allowed her to stroke the back of her head. The cat purred.

"You look tired," the woman told the cat. "I wish you'd come into the house once in a while. Remember when there were three feet of snow on the ground, and it was almost thirty below? I opened the basement door and put down some food and a bed for you, but you just walked away. Remember that?"

The farmer's wife could feel the love for this cat swelling in her heart. She admired her courage, her independence, and her loyalty. She was beautiful, not ratty and worn down like some barn cats. But she also feared the cat's vulnerability. She knew what happened to barn cats. They simply vanished one day. All of them. There was never a trace. They were just gone. She didn't want that to happen to this cat. She couldn't bear it. This one was special.

She wondered at the very strange relationship that had developed between this wild and undomesticated creature and the dutiful rooster who had watched over his hens and crowed religiously—and loudly—for so many years. Now it was the barn cat who was dutiful, keeping her faithful deathwatch.

The farmer visited the two friends every morning, and his wife came in two or three times during the day and once just before bed. The rooster grew perceptibly weaker, and still the cat didn't leave his side.

Late one night, after the farmer and his wife were asleep and the woods and barns were quiet, the rooster's heartbeat became faint, and he began to struggle for breath. He raised his head to look at his hens, and then at the barn cat beside him. She felt his heart stop and his breathing quiet. Almost instantly, his body began to grow cold. She felt a strange, unfamiliar sensation, unease that was almost like sadness, isolation that was almost like loneliness.

Then she stood up, hopped onto one of the wooden beams that held the hay, and leapt up onto one of the bales. With no time to brace herself, she soared straight up into the air and caught a barn swallow in full flight, the bird stunned and in her mouth before it even noticed her presence.

She jumped back down and dropped the dead bird down onto the ground near the rooster's head.

THE NEXT MORNING, the farmer's wife came in with some oatmeal—the temperature had plunged to fifteen degrees. The old rooster was dead, stretched out on the wooden pallet, his eyes closed. The cat was still pressed against him, as if passing him her warmth. A foot away was a dead barn swallow, stiff and cold. The cat turned to watch the woman.

The farmer's wife disappeared into a corner of the barn and returned with a shovel and a garbage bag. She scooped up the rooster and the bird and deposited them both into the bag.

She looked over at the cat. "What did you do? Bring him a gift?" She smiled and shook her head. Then she carried the bag out to the trash heap, which her husband would later collect with his tractor and dump into a hole in the back of the pasture. The coyotes and vultures and other scavengers would make quick work of the rooster's carcass.

When she returned to the barn, she sat down near the cat with the steaming bowl of oatmeal. "Good job," she told the cat, who looked up at her, then padded over to sniff at the oatmeal. The cat was disoriented; she seemed to be looking around for the rooster, waiting for him to appear. She meowed, as if calling out for him.

"You'll miss your friend," the farmer's wife told the cat. She isn't likely to find another, not the way she lives, she thought silently.

"You can come into the house anytime you want," the woman said. "Your life is hard and you've done enough."

The cat came over and sniffed her hand, but when the farmer's wife reached for her, she vanished into the dark stacks of square bales.

Ernie and the Bottled-Water Contest

From her Pharma-Rite cashier station, Karen could peer out the door and look across the highway—through the whizzing trucks and cars—to her aging blue Corolla. She couldn't actually see Ernie, her noisy five-year-old Boston terrier (though often she could hear his distinctive high-pitched barking), or Napoleon, her imperious orange tabby; they were tucked away on their beds in the animal encampment in the rear of the car.

But she believed they could see her, and thus know she was all right. She knew Ernie worried about her when they were apart.

Sometimes when her boss, Jim, the assistant manager of the store, was in the storeroom or taking delivery of some orders, she would run out into the parking lot so her "guys" could see her more clearly. Or to make sure they were safe. In the summer, she parked the car in shade and left the windows open (she had a portable fan working from the backseat on particularly hot days), and in the winter, she always parked in the sun. Despite these precautions, she couldn't help looking in on them a few times a day. She felt guilty about leaving the animals out in the car.

At times, when she thought nobody was listening, and even when she knew they were, she would yodel at Ernie from the edge of the highway. "Hey, Ernie, odel-odel-lay-he-hooo!" she would warble. It was their secret signal, a distinctive sound he could pick up on. She didn't have a sound for Napoleon the cat. But cats didn't really need that kind of reassurance.

The yodeling brought surprised and sometimes disapproving stares from people driving by and from customers in the store parking lot, but Karen, a wiry, brown-haired woman with a leathery face and bright green eyes, was not bothered. If they were dog people, they would understand. And if they were not, then she didn't care what they thought anyway. Ernie was her heart, pure and simple.

The girls working next to her teased her mercilessly whenever she went outside to check on Ernie and Napoleon. "You got a guy out there? You can't be waving to a dog!" they would jeer, but she just laughed them off.

It was clear that Ernie and Napoleon disliked each other. Ernie growled whenever the cat came near him, and the cat spent most of the day hissing at the dog. He was a worthless intruder in her eyes. (Yes, *her* eyes. Karen was constantly explaining to people that she knew Napoleon Bonaparte was a man, but she hadn't known it when she named the cat and wasn't about to change her name now.)

Napoleon disliked riding in cars almost as much as she disliked Ernie. But Karen made her come so Ernie would have company out there in the Corolla. Even if they didn't like each other, at least they weren't alone. She imagined they brought some comfort to each other. And Napoleon did at least like sunning herself through the back window.

IT WAS THE FIRST DAY of the Pharma-Rite Regional Bottled-Water Contest. Karen had come to work at three thirty A.M., even though her shift didn't start until five. She put on a crisp blue Pharma-Rite vest and checked out the twelve cases of bottled water she had undertaken to sell that week. Each case had twelve bottles—she had a lot to move. The contest began at eight A.M.; no sales before that counted. The winner got a good crack at promotion to department manager, and Karen was hoping to get Cosmetics, one of the busiest departments in the store.

She came in at four A.M. most mornings to sort out the shelves—it was unbelievable how people liked to pick things up and put them down in the wrong place. "Slobs," she muttered. Would they do that at home? Put dish soap in the linen closet or a towel in the refrigerator? But she loved that quiet time in the store, tidying up, checking stock, getting the place ready to open. Once the doors opened at six A.M., she worked the drive-thru window where people on their way to work dropped off their prescriptions in the plastic pneumatic tubes.

Most of the jobs at Pharma-Rite were pretty much by the numbers, as easily done by teenagers as adults. That was why the turnover was so high and the pay so low. But at the drive-thru, she got to chat with people and even see their dogs once in a while. She kept a box of biscuits by her chair and always tucked one in the tube when there was a dog in the car. She knew a bunch of the pet owners by name, or at least by the names of their dogs.

She had some regulars she looked forward to seeing—Spinner, the border collie; Tar, the black Lab; and Wrigley, the golden, were among her favorites. She told their owners about Ernie, and how she wished he could be in the back parking lot where he would be closer. He would enjoy seeing the other dogs, she knew, even if he did bark at every dog he saw. And every person.

Halfway through her shift she switched to the front-of-store cashier stations. She had fun up front too. She always tried to make some small talk with the customers. She had a good word or thought for everybody, little bright spots to help people get through long and tough days. Warrensburg was a poor town in the Adirondacks, and the faces of many of the people she saw were tired, worn. If she could get a smile out of someone, it was a good thing.

At the checkout counter, Karen wielded her wand like a maestro's at the symphony. She almost danced around the things people bought—the jars of lotion, Band Aids and tissues, medications and stationery. She knew just how to angle the wand to scan the price, and she prided herself on her thoughtful and efficient packing of those shapeless plastic bags. When she said, "Have a good day," she meant it, and she loved to say something nice about the scarves, pins, or hairstyles of the older women who came in to get their prescriptions filled. Most of them smiled and nodded. The teen customers were hopeless—they didn't interact with her in any way. She just wished them all a safe and happy day.

Karen had enjoyed swiping credit cards before Pharma-

Rite installed the new machines that allowed the customers to swipe their own cards. Truth was, she liked it when the electronic cash system went down—which it did frequently—and you actually had to look at the prices of things and talk to people. She noticed that the kids who worked in the store moved from one automated job to another, reading instructions off screens. They didn't really know how to talk to people. They let the wands do their talking and thinking, and barely muttered the required "Have a good day." That was a shame, Karen thought.

Sometimes, waving the wand back and forth, she felt like a robot with no real reason to know the products or talk to humans. She always asked people if they'd found what they wanted, or if she could help them in any way, but customers would keep coming to the Pharma-Rite even if she didn't. The company had recently installed a fully automated checkout system that digitally tallied shoppers' purchases. The total—reduced by a 15 percent discount—flashed on a screen, and the customer paid with a swiped credit card. People bagged their stuff themselves. Karen had no doubt that that was the future, but she fought the idea that companies no longer cared about people and people no longer cared about companies. You make your own story, she kept telling herself. And she cared.

Karen worked to remain outgoing and helpful. Since the recession, more and more people came to Pharma-Rite to ask health questions and buy over-the-counter medications. They couldn't afford to go see doctors or fill prescriptions. The staff wasn't supposed to give out medical advice, but sometimes you really couldn't help it. Karen would suggest skin creams, effective headache medications, and the stuff that seemed to work for colds, flu, eczema, sore joints. Rather than recommend medicines outright, which was a fireable offense, she simply said it worked for her.

And she had a special radar for the dog people. When customers saw the locket with Ernie's photo hanging from her necklace, they would often take out their cell phones and show her pictures of their own dogs or cats. She liked that. Her cell had a dozen photos of Ernie, and she could whip it out as fast as anybody.

Karen had started bringing Ernie to work over a year ago. His obsessive barking was driving the neighbors crazy, and they had threatened to call the police. Karen wasn't about to crate him (like that would keep him from barking anyway) or use one of those anti-barking spray collars, even though the vet said it was perfectly safe. Her husband, Dan, who thought Ernie was a dreadful pain in the ass, said they couldn't leave him alone in the house any longer.

This annoyed Karen for several reasons. A year earlier, Dan had suffered a mild heart attack. Minutes before it happened, Ernie had started to bark furiously. It was obvious to Karen that Ernie had sensed something was wrong and was trying to warn Dan. But her husband was unappreciative, even ungrateful. "Karen," he scoffed, "that dog barks at everything."

Since then, Karen had watched Ernie's reaction to people closely, and she firmly believed he could sense things others couldn't. She had read about dogs who could sniff out cancer, predict death, warn of strokes. About dogs who saw right through people, who were spiritual and profound. She truly believed Ernie might be one of those dogs. She had faith in him, and believed she alone understood what he was trying to communicate.

But despite Ernie's special gifts, Dan would not back down about leaving the dog alone in the house. So Karen had rearranged the back of the car, laid out dog and cat beds, bones and catnip toys, water and snacks. Ernie could bark all he wanted in the parking lot across from the store, and nobody would care. On her breaks and lunch hour, she would go out and visit the "odd couple," as she called them, walking Ernie and letting Napoleon sit on the hood of the car, where she glowered at the world.

KAREN'S FIRST CUSTOMER of the day was a school-bus driver getting some groceries from Pharma-Rite's new "Food Corner." He bought a six-pack of beer, two packs of bubble gum, two glazed donuts, barbecue potato chips, an apple wrapped in cellophane, six $3 lottery tickets, and a pack of cigarettes.

"And do you have any Tums?" he asked.

"Duh!" muttered Karen under her breath, but he didn't hear her.

Sometimes, when she was out of earshot of the bosses, she joked that she had figured out Pharma-Rite's secret corporate strategy: Sell a lot of chips, hot dogs, candy, cigarettes, and beer so that people would come in for prescriptions when they got fat and sick. There was no health-food department at this pharmacy.

"Should we be selling cigarettes?" she would ask Jim, who just shrugged and said it was up to Corporate. Jim was not a guy to question Corporate. He was a large nervous man who desperately tried to keep up with the stream of regulations, ideas, and cost-saving strategies from Corporate. They never stopped coming.

Truth was, prescriptions were only a small part of what

Pharma-Rite was about these days—they sold food, toys, cosmetics, soaps and detergents, you name it. Even pet food and toys.

"Hey, can I interest you in some of our new bottled water?" Karen asked the bus driver.

"No," he said groggily. "I don't buy water."

That was sort of the tone of things. She wasn't selling many bottles.

Karen was lucky to have her cashier's job. She needed it. But she was also fearful about her future. Employees were entitled to health-care benefits after four years at Pharma-Rite, and Karen, along with everybody else, noticed that people tended to get laid off or downsized right before their benefits kicked in. Any kid off the street could perform most of the jobs at Pharma-Rite with little training and less pay. Why keep on the employees who had earned benefits?

Karen was in her fourth year at the store, and life was catching up—her mother was sick, Dan's legs were getting worse, and jobs were vanishing as fast as the ozone layer. She needed to get one of the department-manager slots that the company was posting. The Warrensburg store was one of the smaller ones in the region, dwarfed by the volume done in Saratoga or Glens Falls. That's why the Pharma-Rite Regional Bottled-Water Contest was looming large for Karen, and for her boss, Jim.

The company was launching its own bottled-water brand. Part of the sales push was the contest. Employees who sold the most bottled water that week went to the top of the list for promotion. And Karen was going for it. Walmart wasn't hiring, and the only other jobs around were eighty miles down the thruway in Saratoga, and there weren't many of those.

In their apartment in Hudson Falls, Karen had been driving Dan crazy practicing various sales pitches, getting her voice "up," and memorizing the company pamphlets extolling the miraculous benefits of their clean, pure water. It had to be better than beer and cigarettes, she thought, practicing one of her pitches on Ernie.

She'd adopted the dog at a local Adirondack animal shelter after some summer people abandoned him outside the cottage they had rented, just dumped him out on the road. A neighbor saw them do it and could hardly believe it. He called in their license-plate number. A trooper actually pulled them over on the New York State Thruway heading to New Jersey. "What dog?" they said. They might have seen one wandering around, but they knew nothing about it. It wasn't theirs. There was nothing the trooper could do. Maybe Ernie's abandonment explained why he was so verbal, so indignant. Perhaps he was still seething at the injustices done to him.

"Their loss, my gain," Karen said of the awful people who had abandoned Ernie. She and the dog had bonded instantly, and she brought him everywhere but the doctor's office and her mother's nursing home. She loved him to death, and he had become pretty much a one-human dog. He was either with Karen or barking in protest that he wasn't with Karen.

"Ernie," she had told him that morning, "I need to win this contest. Get that promotion. Get us noticed by Corporate." She didn't want to be one of the many checkout girls who vanished from Pharma-Rite after four years. She wanted to make it past that expiration date. She wanted to get benefits, better pay, and some job security, if such a thing even existed. Maybe even get to go to the annual meeting in Fort Meyers, Florida, one day, or win a cruise.

In the locker room, the other girls had wished one another luck as they pulled their hair back in buns and ponytails and put on their blue vests. Karen was competing with Susie from Cosmetics and Jamie, a pill counter in the pharmacy, but her real competitors probably worked at the larger stores in the region. Still, Susie and Jamie were both cute and quite a bit younger than Karen, who was in her mid-forties. They had boyfriends and pals who came by all the time. They might draw more of a crowd than she did.

The first day of the contest was a disaster for Karen. She called Dan on the cell and told him that nobody seemed to want bottled water from Pharma-Rite, even at $5.99 a case. Jamie's boyfriend came into the parking lot on his motorbike and bought a couple of cases. Karen hadn't come close to that. On her break, she had gone out to see the odd couple and walked Ernie around the block. She didn't take him as far as she usually did, wanting to get back and sell some bottles.

Some of her regulars bought a few, but by early afternoon, she had barely sold a case.

Tuesday was not much better. Jim came to check on her numbers and he shook his head. He was nervous, unhappy. "Your competition is outselling you," he said, "and they aren't selling much." Karen prided herself on being upbeat, but Jim was a difficult person for even her to like. He seemed to care about nothing but his faraway bosses and their business goals, and was careful not to get too close to any employees—they might not be around for long. Still, Karen was easy to talk to, and Jim sometimes confided a bit in her. "I'll be honest with you—it would be nice to beat out Saratoga and Glens Falls. Get Corporate to notice us. We aren't exactly their busiest store around here, if you know what I mean."

Karen knew what he meant. Stores that were not the busiest ones often vanished overnight, taking everybody's jobs with them. Jim said the chain's regional manager was a big fan of Chairman Mao of China, and he believed in getting rid of the weakest links every now and then to keep the chain strong. It was a chilling management philosophy, all the more so because Karen knew it was true.

Karen's sister had stopped by and picked up a few bottles, to be nice. Susie gave her a condescending smirk. Everybody knew she wasn't selling any water. If this kept up, she'd have to start looking online for jobs in Saratoga or Lake George. Karen was discouraged, which didn't happen often. Her mother had taught her that being discouraged was like opening up a dark door—it let awful stuff in. You just didn't do it.

On Wednesday morning, Dan called her on the cell to wish her well. "Maybe you can put that useless dog to work," he said. "He drinks a lot of water."

She knew his suggestion had only been a snide joke—he was not a huge fan of Ernie—but it set something off inside her head. She took the dog for a long walk out by the cement plant, where the two of them looked up, as they did every day, at the giant Days Without Accidents or Injuries sign that towered over the neighborhood. The cement plant had not had an accident or injury in more than one thousand days, and that meant something to Karen. She saw the sign as something akin to a spiritual site, a place of safety and stability in the world.

• • •

ON THURSDAYS Karen worked a later shift, four P.M. to midnight, so Jim and the other early employees (she suspected that Jim lived in the office at the back of the store, as she had never seen him come or go, only work) were surprised to see her pull into the Pharma-Rite parking lot at six A.M. She'd left Napoleon at home, and the grumpy cat had seemed more than pleased to stay.

Ernie, however, was sitting in the backseat, yapping away.

She had gussied him up, giving him a bath, which he hated, putting sweet-smelling powder on him, and placing a yellow Hawaiian lei (a souvenir from her sister's last trip to Disney World) around his neck.

Jim frowned. He didn't like dogs in general and Ernie in particular. Company policy and state health laws banned them from the store, and Jim didn't even like them hanging around the parking lot, which is why Karen always parked across the street. Jim insisted that somebody could get bit, or worse, the dog would take a dump—not the image Pharma-Rite wanted to project.

"You can't leave him this close to the store," he said.

Karen motioned for Jim to step aside.

"Listen," she said. "Do you want to win the Regional Bottled-Water Contest or not?"

Jim's eyes widened. It would be a huge coup for a small store in Warrensburg to beat the busier Pharma-Rites in Glens Falls or Saratoga. One of his buddies down at the Glens Falls store had e-mailed him to tell him that Corporate had called to chastise the manager for not pushing the contest. They were ticked about the sluggish sales of their new water line in its first week.

"Just bear with me," said Karen. She went to the stationery section and came out with a blank cardboard poster and some crayons, then went and got Ernie out of the car. He sat barking, wagging his tail.

She scribbled on the poster and then set it up in the parking lot against the rear wall of the store.

"Psychic Dog," it read. "Let Ernie tell your fortune. Free with the purchase of two bottles of water."

Before Jim could close his mouth, there were six people in line.

"Is this for real?" asked a mom with two kids in tow. "I saw a dog like this on Oprah."

"Try it," challenged Karen. "Ask him anything you want to know about your future."

The woman walked up to Ernie, who looked up at her. She glanced back at her kids, closed her eyes, tilted her face toward the sky, and then took a breath.

"Will my husband get a job?" she finally asked. Ernie looked up at her and began to bark.

"Wow," said the woman. "It's like he really listened to me. What did he say?"

Karen forced herself to remind the customer that while the predictions were free, the water wasn't. Two bottles, $2.25.

The woman took out her purse and bought three bottles. Ernie barked at her again.

"So what did he say?" she asked Karen again as her two kids drew in closer.

"Ernie says absolutely. Your husband will definitely get a job."

The woman smiled and one of the kids squealed, "Awesome! Wait until we get home and tell Daddy!"

A truck driver stepped to the front of the line and bought two bottles.

Ernie barked and the driver looked at him dubiously. "I had a mutt who drove with me for ten years," he said. "Looked a little like him."

Karen saw that the man's eyes had filled with tears. "Hey," she asked, "what's your question?"

"Will it cost me more than five hundred dollars to get the transmission on my truck fixed?"

Karen listened to Ernie bark.

"No" said Karen. "Ernie says less than that."

Next, a middle-aged woman came up to the dog, looked him in the eye, and bought a whole case of bottled water. She looked worn. Karen waited while the woman summoned the strength to speak up.

"Will my mother recover from her cancer?" she asked.

This was too much for Jim. Before Karen could say a word, he stepped forward and whispered, "Karen, we can't have this. These people will be furious if the predictions don't come true. They'll come back and sue us."

He tried to give the women her money back, but she put up her hand and looked right into Ernie's eyes. "No," she said, "I want an answer."

Karen listened to Ernie's barks, and then, with a strange look in her eye, threw her arms around the woman and said, "Your mother will recover, at least for a while." The woman burst into tears.

Jim ordered Karen to put Ernie in the car and go home.

She picked up the dog and moved him to the rear seat, muttering under her breath. It wasn't until she was a mile or so from Pharma-Rite that she became terrified she would lose her job.

In fact, she wasn't sure if she'd already been fired or not. Jim hadn't said either way.

Once home, Dan was furious. "How could you do that?" he thundered. "This dog doesn't know squat. He isn't a psychic. He was just shooting his mouth off, like he always does. You're giving these people false hope."

Karen said nothing, but burst into tears. Had she lost her job? Misled people? Lost her mind? It started as a bottled-water contest, and there, out in the parking lot with Ernie, she had kind of lost perspective. But she wasn't lying. She believed Ernie knew more than most dogs. She was sure of it.

She went into her room and put her head on the pillow and cried. She would never get promoted, and couldn't even imagine getting to keep her job. At least Jim hadn't called to fire her yet. He was probably waiting for the morning. Ernie, puzzled, lay on the bed next to her. He was quiet for once. Napoleon looked on disdainfully.

The next morning, Karen got up early, drove to the Pharma-Rite, and left Ernie and Napoleon in the car across the road from the store. She went through the aisles, putting bottles of lotion back in their proper places, picking up the bags of chocolate and cough drops that had been knocked to the floor. Then she took her place at the drive-thru window, and when she was done, reported to her cashier station. Her hands were trembling but there was still no sign of Jim.

Karen looked out the window to see if Ernie was all right and noticed a small commotion in the parking lot. There were about a dozen people there—a big crowd at that hour—and Jim was standing out there in his Pharma-Rite manager's vest trying to placate them. Karen asked her friend Janine to cover her station and stepped outside.

The first person she saw was the mother with her two children. She clapped her hands when she spotted Karen. "My husband got a job yesterday," she said. "Your dog is miraculous. I want to buy some more water."

The truck driver was right behind her. "Me too," he said. "The transmission work cost two hundred fifty. How did the dog do it? I want to ask him about a new car I want to buy." Karen looked around for the woman whose mother had cancer, but she didn't see her.

There was a line now, halfway across the lot. She looked at Jim, who gave her a nod. "I wasn't out here," he said. "In case anybody asks, I was never here. I never saw this." He looked down, shook his head, and retreated inside the store.

Karen crossed the road to her car, got the sign and Ernie, and set up against the rear wall, just like the day before.

She sold out of bottled water by noon. Jim stacked a few more cases. Ernie barked continuously, making a string of predictions: the local high school would win a football championship; a young wife would get pregnant; three women would get married; a boy would move out of his mother's house and live near the ocean; a divorce-court judge would rule in favor of a father's custody plea; a hunter would get some deer. The words just came streaming out of Karen's mouth, and she was sure they were from Ernie. Bottles of water kept selling.

Every now and then Jim would come out with another stack of bottled-water cases, then flee. In the mid-afternoon, he appeared again, practically glowing. "We won. We beat Saratoga and Glens Falls. I get to go to the awards dinner Corporate is giving at the end of the month."

Karen had never seen Jim smile like that.

He reached into his pocket and pulled out an "Employee of the Month" pin, plastic painted to look like brass. He told her she would get the "Employee of the Month" parking spot by the side of the store as well. And, he whispered, she was free to keep Ernie there. He winked, and then said, sotto voce, "Get used to the Cosmetics Department."

By late afternoon, the crowd had dispersed and Karen put Ernie back in the Corolla with Napoleon. She headed into the locker room to change out of her blue vest. When she left the store, the woman who had asked about her mother's cancer was standing alone in the parking lot.

Karen came up to her. "I hope I didn't give you any false hope," she said. "I'm not a doctor. I was up thinking about you all night. It just came out that way—"

The woman smiled. "Last night, I went home and told my mom what the dog had said. She clapped her hands, got up out of bed, and said she wanted to go for a walk. We walked through the park and along the river, and she laughed and had some popcorn and smiled for me, and I will remember that smile for the rest of my life. I wanted to come and thank Ernie for making my mother smile."

Acknowledgments

Thanks to Elizabeth Stein, Rosemary Ahern, Jen Smith, Maria Wulf.

Thanks to the families, farmers, and box-store women who let me into their lives, and allowed me to see what animals mean to them in contemporary America.

PHOTO: MARIA WULF

JON KATZ has written twenty-five books, including works of nonfiction, novels, short stories, and books for children; he is also a photographer. He has written for *The New York Times, The Wall Street Journal,* Slate, *Rolling Stone,* and the *AKC Gazette* and has worked for CBS News, *The Boston Globe, The Washington Post,* and *The Philadelphia Inquirer.* He lives on Bedlam Farm, in upstate New York, with his wife, the artist Maria Wulf, and their dogs, donkeys, barn cats, sheep, and chickens.

About the Type

This book was set in Baskerville, a typeface which was designed by John Baskerville, an amateur printer and typefounder, and cut for him by John Handy in 1750. The type became popular again when The Lanston Monotype Corporation of London revived the classic Roman face in 1923. The Mergenthaler Linotype Company in England and the United States cut a version of Baskerville in 1931, making it one of the most widely used typefaces today.